CW00920526

ChangelingPress.com

Blood/ Stryker Duet

Marteeka Karland

Blood/ Stryker Duet

Marteeka Karland

ISBN: 978-1-60521-804-5

Publisher:
Changeling Press LLC
315 N. Centre St.
Martinsburg, WV 25404
ChangelingPress.com

Printed in the U.S.A.

Editor: Katriena Knights
Cover Artist: Marteeka Karland, Angela Knight

The individual stories in this anthology have been
previously released in E-Book format.

Table of Contents

Blood (Salvation's Bane MC 5)

Marteeka Karland

Alizay -- My life is complicated enough without the big biker mercenary I'm tasked with helping to rehabilitate. He's not a fan of physical therapy and I'm not a fan of the way I react to his body. Nothing in my life could have prepared me for the man called Blood. He's crass, stubborn, and so sexy it actually hurts. If I'm going to resist him I've got to be strong. I'm just not sure any woman is strong enough to ignore him when he decides he doesn't want to be ignored.

Blood -- I'm the one who cleans up the messes made by others. Then she comes along and suddenly I'm the mess. She thinks she's leaving when she's done with me, but I've got other plans for little Alizay. She's going to be mine whether she wants to or not. Her past may stand in our way, but that doesn't mean I'm going to give up.

With Christmas on the way and me dragging out my recovery in order to get some quality time with my sexy therapist, my club and my team decide to bring Christmas to me. Bones, Salvation's Bane, and the Shadow Demons. All under one roof. What could possibly go wrong?

Chapter One

"One more pass through the city. Then I'm calling it."

It took everything in Blood not to roll his eyes at the order. Salvation's Bane had teamed with Bones to help out the Shadow Demons. Waste of fucking time if you asked him. Cain, the president of Bones, was also their boss at ExFil, the paramilitary organization most members of Bones and Bane belonged to. The client was also close with ExFil, supplying most of the company's tech -- and ExFil had some shit. Cain might be Blood's boss, but Thorn was his president.

Cain had called them all -- Bones and Salvation's Bane -- here as bikers. Not military. By that way of thinking, Blood should be taking orders from Thorn. Not Cain. They might be sister clubs, but Blood had a fiercely dominant streak that made it nearly impossible for him to follow just anyone. While he respected Cain, Blood wasn't a member of Bones. Never had been, though he'd ridden with them for a time out of necessity to Cain and ExFil. He was Salvation's Bane, and Bane was a little grittier than Bones. Probably because Thorn didn't own a multi-million-dollar company full of mercenaries. They did, however, own two fitness centers, two strip clubs, and a BDSM club. Fuckin' A.

"Fuck," he muttered as he revved his bike once before taking off with the rest of the group.

"I'm with you, brother," Stryker said beside him.

"As if anyone with any Goddamned sense wouldn't hide from a group of fuckin' bikers rollin' down the fuckin' block over and over." Blood was fed up. Restless. He hated not knowing what the fuck was going on.

"That's because you ain't trying to spot anyone, dipshits," Cain's voice snapped. "You're here to be spotted. You got a problem with bein' called dipshits, don't bitch like a couple of pussies into a hot fuckin' mic."

Ouch.

"Yeah, rookie move," Blood admitted. He still sounded disgruntled.

"Which is why you're not privy to the greater goal. Now get your fuckin' heads outta your asses and keep an eye on our six, Tail Gunner," Cain said, reminding Blood he was in charge of making sure everything was safe at the back of the formation.

They'd been doing this for the better part of four fucking days. Apparently, Shadow Demons had hired ExFil to do a job for them. The Shadow Demons were complicated. They weren't an MC, but they operated in a similar manner. Just with more money. *Way* more money. This same scenario had happened a few times, but it was always shrouded in secrecy with no clear goal. Last time, they'd rescued a child from some tunnels beneath the city of Rockwell where the more unsavory elements ruled and authorities couldn't penetrate. Blood hadn't been part of that, but he had returned for the clean-up. This mission was as secretive as the other one, only this time Blood was right in the thick of it. Every available member of both Salvation's Bane and Bones were out in full force on this one.

"Might help if we actually knew what we're lookin' for, Top," Blood said, referring to Cain as "Top" because he was in charge of the mission -- the commanding officer.

"That's need to know, and you don't. I'll fuckin' tell you when we fuckin' find it."

If Blood got out of this with his fuckin' sanity intact, he was resigning from ExFil. Fuck this fucking shit. Which was why he couldn't help but goad the other man.

"Which means Demons ain't told you shit. Kinda reminds me of last time. Seem to remember hearin' 'bout someone tellin' Alex it was bullshit then, and that it wasn't happenin' again. Guess we all know how that worked out."

The silence on the other end was deafening. More than one of Salvation's Bane fist-bumped as they rode in tight formation. More than one of Bones gave him deadly looks over their shoulders. Blood couldn't give a good Goddamn. He believed in calling bullshit out when it was needed. This was clearly the time.

Blood snorted like he'd won the round. He knew that was bullshit too. Cain would likely throw him a beating later. Or at least he'd try. Blood didn't pull punches. Ever.

The weather was growing colder as summer faded to autumn. Leaves littered the road in places even in the heart of the city. Despite the urban sprawl that was Rockwell, the place was missing the haze of smog most cities this size had. Thanks to Argent Tech, the company owned by Shadow Demons, Rockwell boasted some of the most brilliant minds in the world, as well as all the comforts and luxuries of any major city. And just like in any major city, crime was sometimes a problem. In the poorer sections, but also the white-collar sections. Which was where they were now. Which meant they stuck out like bikers on fucking Wall Street.

It made little sense to Blood. Their presence would likely inflame any real problems in this area. They weren't going to intimidate anyone here. They'd only make someone want to strike from the shadows. It made Blood nervous, and Blood never put himself in situations where he got nervous.

"Need to know when I'm in charge of the rear and there's a bigass fuckin' target on our backs in flashing neon fuckin' orange, Cain. Why are we setting ourselves up as a fuckin' target?"

"Switch over," Cain snapped, indicating for Blood, Thorn, and Carnage, the road captain for Salvation's Bane and the man acting as road captain for them all today, to switch to their private channel. There was a brief silence before Cain came over his earpiece. "You're aware Argent Tech supplies the 'smart' in smart weapons, right?"

"Yeah." Blood had been briefed just like everyone else. "They're the top suppliers for shit to the U.S. and allies all over the world. So?"

"They're also a civilian corporation, surrounded by civilian urban areas. They have great security, but the city only has what the city allows."

"Cain, if Alex and his men think there is a threat to the city, shouldn't we be, you know, just a tad more armed?" Blood was pissed off. More than he wanted to admit. His responsibility was the safety of the club on the road. "I can't keep the men safe if I don't know about this shit!"

"You think I don't know that?" Cain sounded just as eager to pick a fight as Blood felt. "It was part of the contract. Part I'm breaking by telling you this, but…"

"But you've got the same fuckin' feelin' I've got," Blood finished. "Like somethin's out there just waitin' for us."

"Yeah."

"Then why're we still fuckin' out here? At the very least, we need weapons more than sidearms. We need body armor at the very least. Fuck!"

"Why do you think you had to change clothes? Because these have a pretty Shadow Demons emblem on 'em? No! Because it's special body armor. We've all got on armor worth a couple mil a piece. Most advanced and proficient energy absorption and disbursement in the world. Every member of my team is as protected as they can be, other than weaponry, and Demons have that covered."

"So they say."

"So I say! You think I'd leave my men without protection?" Cain was obviously not happy, but whether it was because Blood was calling him out or because of the shit deal he'd agreed to, Blood had no idea and didn't really care.

"Well, you sent us out without all the intel. What the fuck else am I supposed to think?"

"The Demons didn't want it getting out there were probably terrorists in the city."

"And rolling out a fuckin' huge-ass MC, armed to the fuckin' teeth, was a way of keeping that hidden?"

"Alright, Blood," Thorn said, shutting Blood down. "That's enough. I told Cain it was a shit deal, but Shadow Demons wouldn't budge. They said they had their reasons, and he believes them. Frankly, so do I. Those men are fuckin' smart when it comes to this shit."

"And we're not? We analyze and act on intel all over the world through ExFil." Blood had difficulty letting this go. Probably because he was responsible for two clubs instead of one, and it was making him super paranoid.

"Not here we don't," Thorn clarified. "They know this city and its people better than anyone else. If they say this is the best way to handle it, it is." Thorn sighed. "Look, I feel your pain, brother. But the reason Alex called us all in was because he knew there was no one else anywhere who had a better chance of pulling this off. He knows we're deadly as fuck and strong as iron. He's counting on us, and we won't let him down."

Blood wasn't really mollified, but at least he was better informed. "Is there anything else we need to know that we're not allowed to know? Because the longer we're out here the more exposed I'm feeling."

"Only that our job is to draw them out. Alex believes our presence alone would be enough because, though we look like MC, we don't act it so much."

"What the fuck does that mean?" Blood ground his teeth.

"Beats the fuck outta me," Cain said. "We're supposed to let the bad guys know we're on to them. That's what our presence signals. We're making ourselves a target so they can think they have us, but when we come out on the other side and hold our ground, they'll fall back."

"Or just go get stronger ordnance," Blood muttered. "This is still bullshit."

"I know," Cain acknowledged. "OK? I know. I trust Azriel, and Alex by extension. Azriel and I have been through a lot together. If he says he needs this and needs it this way, I'm gonna help him."

"Even to the point of putting your men -- your club -- at risk?" It was the harshest thing Blood could have said. It didn't just border on insubordination, it was grounds for an ass-beating. Normally, Blood wouldn't have gone this far, no matter what he thought, but the whole fucking situation stank like pig shit.

"You and I will discuss this at length. Later," Cain finally said, his voice soft and deadly. "Switch over." That was the end of the discussion. Despite feeling like he'd won, or at least gotten his point across, Blood didn't feel like it had been a victory. He felt like they were all going to lose, and that Cain had known it from the outset. So why agree to it?

Before he could change his channel, Carnage weighed in. Because he was the road captain, he was in charge of the ride as a whole while Blood was responsible for guarding the rear and keeping an eye on the group from his vantage point. Safety was always his number-one priority. "I'll be in on that discussion, too, Top." That was all the backing he needed.

They rode on in silence for the better part of an hour. The route they took altered every round, but took them over every single street in the city. It looked like they were riding at random, but the route had been carefully planned and scouted ahead of time. Blood was exaggerating when he'd implied they had no intel. They did. Just not enough. To his way of thinking, anyone hiring a man to throw his body out there to shield someone else had the right to have all the details. That included who they were looking for and why. Whether it was a local group or more of an international sect, he wanted to know about it.

They were on the last third of a round when Blood noticed something on a high building above them. The day was overcast so very little sunlight filtered through the clouds, but for the briefest moment, the sun shone down on the exact spot he needed to see the danger.

"Two o'clock! Eighth-story balcony window!" he barked. "RPG!"

The second the words were out, he saw the flash and smoke as the weapon was discharged. Seconds later, an explosion rocked the group. Blood saw most of the men scatter, getting out of the line of fire, but one bike went flying, its rider tossed off to the side.

Blood skidded to a stop, barely getting the kickstand down before he jumped off, headed toward his brother from Bones. Surprisingly, Sword rolled twice before coming to a crouch in the road, seemingly unharmed. Blood helped him to his feet and the two of them ran just as another explosion knocked them off their feet. Blood expected the pain to hit him any second, but it never came.

He pushed up and glanced around him.

Sword had headed back into the smoking craters in the road, calling out for the men who'd been beside him. Vicious and Viper, from Salvation's Bane and Bones respectively, were also off their bikes but didn't seem to be hurt. Instead they crouched in the middle of the road behind the wreckage that had been their bikes and took aim at the building Blood had identified as the target.

Amazingly, none of the ExFil men called out an injury. A couple of them were obviously shell shocked, but rapidly getting their bearings and pulling weapons. Blood spotted two civilians on the sidewalk pressed against the brick building. The young male covered the female with his body, pressing her against the wall as best he could, shielding his head with his hands, her head with his body. Blood quickly moved to them and helped them around the corner and into a storefront before making his way back to his men.

Weapon tracking where he'd seen the attack, Blood was itching for a target to kill. He'd missed Cain's order to fire or hold when he'd been blasted off his feet, but there was no way he'd hold them off. Except there were civilians all over the fucking place. Blood swore loudly as he skidded to a stop beside Sword and Shadow.

"We got a target?" His breath came in gasps and his ears still rang, but his hands were steady.

"Bastards pulled up and moved," Sword growled. "Look." He pointed to the window where Blood had first seen their adversary. A tracking laser glowed against the partially open window, but that was it.

"What's going on?" Was someone getting ready to fire?

"Not sure. Cain said to stand by unless we have a clear target. Can't imagine anyone would shoot into a window in the middle of the city, but then again, I never expected to be attacked like this either." Sword gave him a wry grin. "I guess the fuckin' body armor works, huh?"

"Seems like." Blood keyed his mic. "Anyone not accounted for? Do we need a sound-off?"

"I accounted for everyone but you," Carnage said. "Body armor held. We're good --"

Carnage hadn't finished his sentence when another massive explosion knocked Blood off his feet. His foot somehow got caught, probably between the bike he was crouched behind and the pavement, and he felt something give way. Agony shot from his right knee to his hip. Somehow, he was still conscious and managed not to cry out.

Blood considered himself pretty stoic. He'd been shot before. Had broken bones. But nothing had ever hurt as much as this. He felt like his leg had been ripped off his body. Every move he made, even breathing hurt. Somewhere in his chaotic mind, he registered Sword beside him with Shadow and Vicious. All three men were dragging him away from their cover and toward the building.

Cain was shouting something and there was another explosion. Strangely, Blood didn't feel the concussion from the blast this time. Dust and smoke filled the air, so thick he was choking on it. There were screams of men and women all around him. It sounded like a fucking war zone, not a city street.

"What the fuck have they done?" Sword bit out. "This whole fuckin' block is toast! There are people all over the place!"

"I thought your buddies knew what they were doin', Cain?" Thorn snapped over the comm. "What the fuck?"

"That's not the Demons," Cain said. "Those were set at the foot of the building giving us fire. Deliberately demolished."

"EMS is on the way." Blood thought that was one of the Shadow Demons over the radio, but he wasn't sure. The pain was so intense he was having trouble focusing. "Need anyone you can spare to assist there, Cain."

"Fuck," the man muttered.

"Fucking hell! Is everyone here? Blood needs immediate medical attention!" That was Shadow. The big African-American was trying to pry off Blood's body armor. What had been once been as flexible as a T-shirt was now stiff as fucking steel. Shadow swore as he pulled and tried to force the material away from Blood, but it wouldn't budge. "Someone tell me how to get this fuckin' shit off him! I need to see how bad he's hurt!"

Blood could have told him it was pretty fucking bad. But the more Shadow and Sword tried to work with the armor, the worse it hurt. It wasn't long before the edges of Blood's vision blurred. The pain was so bad now he couldn't scream even if he'd wanted to. Every movement of his leg took any breath he might have used, so he didn't have breath to spare to scream.

He closed his eyes, trying to find the calm that was so easy for him to hold on to in battle. It was there, but the pain was unrelenting. There seemed to be no ease on it. It was like that fucking body armor was holding his leg in an unnatural position, creating the unbearable, stabbing pain in his hip and thigh.

Blood heard his brothers readying for battle. Blindly, he reached for his sidearm, trying to chamber a round. Someone grabbed the weapon from his hands, not bothering to explain.

The next thing he saw was the most angelic, beautiful face he'd ever had the pleasure of viewing. As before, when he'd first noticed the threat looming over him, the sun shone on the woman leaning over him. Her golden hair gleamed as she moved, looking much like a halo around her head. Impossibly pale skin was stained with pink on her cheeks. Her hand brushed over his face, pulling off his helmet. Everywhere her skin touched his was like silk over his rough skin.

"We're going to get you out of here," she said, her voice melodious and strong. Blood reached for her wrist weakly when she pulled away. His big hand circled her delicate arm with room to spare. Was she a child? She reached for his chest and did something with her free hand. Immediately, the armor relaxed around him and his leg moved back to a more relaxed position. The pain was still there, but not the sharp, constant agony from before. She immediately stuffed what he thought was a trauma dressing over the leg she'd just bared, pressing down hard. Pain exploded down the limb as she did.

"What did you do?" He managed to bite out, his voice barely above a whisper and so hoarse he hardly recognized himself.

"Sometimes, the material gets stuck," she explained, sounding like she was oversimplifying the process but repeating it as it had been told to her. "You have to release it. So I did."

Blood wanted to ask her how, but now that the pain had ebbed somewhat, he was crashing. Hard. Try as he might, he couldn't focus on the woman. All he managed to croak out was, "What's your name?"

When she smiled, it was like the heavens had opened up and welcomed him with arms wide. "Alizay," she said. Blood let out a breath he hadn't realized he'd been holding. When he did, the edges of his vision closed in, and he knew no more.

Chapter Two

Alizay had fought her way to the group of men her employers had hired to flush out what they assumed were terrorists out to penetrate the Argent Tech facility. They weren't terrorists. They were businessmen in the city who thought they could hire hooligans to scare employees into letting them in to get specs and blueprints and whatever in order to get their piece of the pie. Sounded a bit far-fetched, and totally not the way to go about such things, but when Daniel J. Madison II had made his attempt to merge his company, Rush Developments, with Argent Tech's robotics splinter and had then disappeared, it had concerned many in the city's elite. Compound that with other recent attempts to take over Argent being met with deadly circumstances, and the men in the city's leading businesses had gotten spooked in a huge way.

Some had pooled their resources and bought mercenaries. Not very good mercenaries, but mercenaries nonetheless. If word around the office was to be believed, several employees had been approached by thugs and threatened or bribed into releasing information. What no one recognized, and everyone failed to believe, was that no one had a fucking clue what Argent Tech did other than their founders and governing board. All this attack had done was hurt property and people. As well as the average person's faith in the city's management.

Alizay didn't know much about the tech coming out of Argent, but she was very familiar with the armor. As the company nurse, she saw many of the training accidents and knew how to remove the stuff in the event of an emergency.

Once she'd pulled the armor away from the man's body, she saw the problem. The armor had caught his leg and held it fast. Probably because he'd been knocked off his feet. She'd seen it happen from time to time, though not this badly. It looked like his upper body had gone one way and his leg had been held stationary, not allowing him to spin with the natural movement. His hip has been dislocated and, unless she missed her guess, the muscles and tendons badly torn. In fact, she wouldn't be surprised if the only thing holding his leg on was his skin. Already there was heavy bruising all around his hip and pelvis. A huge gash where the edge of the malfunctioning armor had caught his leg bled freely. She had no idea if he'd nicked a major vessel, but, if he had, any damage was minimal given he hadn't bled out yet.

"We need to get him to the Argent Tech compound. Fast." Alizay looked at the huge, dark-skinned man guarding her patient.

"Who the fuck are you?" he snapped at her, clearly unwilling to do anything she suggested.

"I'm a nurse at Argent Tech. The bosses have a trauma surgeon there."

"Are you fuckin' kiddin' me? A fuckin' trauma surgeon? At a factory?"

"Argent Tech is much more than a factory," she said, bristling. Though he had a valid question. She didn't know exactly what the company did any more than the people who actually worked with the technical equipment.

"Cain," the other man shouted into the radio. "Got a girl here who wants to move Blood." There was a beat of silence. "To Argent. She got his body armor off. Says she works there." Longer pause this time. "Copy that. Cage is comin' around the back."

Seconds later, a Humvee skidded to a stop inches from them, but blocking the three of them from the street. There hadn't been any more explosions or any gunfire, but no one was taking any chances. The door opened and another man jumped out. He opened the back door and pulled out a canvas stretcher.

"He hurt bad?"

"Fuckin' leg's fucked all to shit and back. Movin' him's gonna be a fuckin' disaster."

"Do you have a slider board?" When she spoke, both men looked at Alizay, their gazes laser sharp.

The one from the Humvee shook his head slowly. "No, but I have a big-ass cardboard box."

"That'll do," she said, leaving the men to fetch what she needed. While she waited for them to retrieve the box and unfold it, she started an IV on the opposite side from her patient's injury and hooked up a bag of fluids.

Without instruction from her, the men carefully shoved the cardboard under their comrade and eased him onto the makeshift stretcher. He moaned, but stayed unconscious. Alizay thought about giving him morphine for his pain, but was hesitant to do it while he was out of it. If he woke up, she'd revisit that question. Right now, she needed to get him somewhere he could be helped. There was absolutely nothing more she could do here.

It took a little time for the two huge men to load him into the back of the vehicle and speed off. Alizay was thankful the bulk of the attack seemed to have stopped, but wasn't optimistic it would stay that way.

"How much further?" They were going faster than she was comfortable with, but the silence was making her nervous. Her guy didn't appear to be declining, but she absolutely had to say something to fill the void.

"Three minutes," the driver muttered. Then he seemed to activate his line of communication. "Did you let Alex and Azriel know we're coming? I don't want a hassle at the gate. Fuckers are probably locked down to fuck and back."

To her surprise, a voice came over the vehicle radio. Apparently they weren't opposed to her listening to them. "They're watchin' for you. Gate should open at your approach."

"Ain't slowin' down. Alex says this thing's as strong as a tank. They don't open, we're about to put that to the test."

True to his word, the driver didn't ease off the gas even a little as they approached the Argent Tech compound. Thankfully, his buddy had been right. The gate slid open at their approach. She watched it sliding close before they rounded the first corner inside the campus.

"Where we headed?"

Before Alizay could open her mouth, the radio started again. "Center building. About two klicks inside. Stay on the main road. Sending GPS to your system."

"I know where to go," she said softly. "As you get close, I can show you where to enter."

"You just worry about Blood. I'll get us where we need to go."

"That's his name? Blood?"

"Got a problem with it?" The man was obviously stressed so she didn't take it personally. Instead of answering, she focused on her patient.

Had he not been covered in grime and mud, he'd have been handsome. He had a full beard, neatly trimmed but heavy, like a lot of the military men seemed to wear them now. It was a dark brown with deep auburn highlights. His hair didn't seem to have any red in it, though both his beard and hair had liberal amounts of silver, especially around the temples and chin. Lines fanned out around his eyes, mouth, and just in front of his ears as if he had some age on him. As she pulled off the rest of the body armor, she noted a heavily muscled physique. In another situation, she'd have marveled at him. So strong and rugged. The perfect specimen of a man.

Not long after she finished inspecting him for other wounds -- finding none -- they pulled into the building and continued until they reached an elevator at the end of the parking garage. Alizay moved so the men could easily get to him when they opened the back of the vehicle. Several men in similar dress were waiting on them with what sounded like several more vehicles heading into the parking garage. They moved Blood's stretcher from the Humvee to a gurney, raising the rails and slamming down the pedal that disengaged the brakes. The elevator seemed to open just in time and all of them filed into it. The big African-American man grabbed her arm and pulled her in with them.

There was nothing Alizay could do until they got to the holding area other than monitor him and make sure he didn't die. The ride down, deeper into the basement of the building, seemed to take forever, though they only went down six sub-levels.

The door opened and they were met by a doctor she didn't know.

"What do we have?" His question was clipped, just as Alizay expected. She'd heard that tone many times before. As she filled him in on the injuries she knew of, the doctor did his own exam, coming to the same conclusion she had. Any other injury he might have could wait until they'd taken care of his hip and leg.

"Did you give him anything for pain?"

"No. He lost consciousness soon after I released the body armor. His pressure has held steady, so I just gave him fluids."

"Good job." He looked up to the men, who were continuing to file into the open room. "I'll keep everyone informed. Expect this to take a while."

That was it. Alizay wasn't a surgical nurse, and this doctor obviously had his own staff, so she was done. Despite having been in emergent situations before, she found herself starting to tremble with the aftereffects of adrenaline hitting her system. It was more the combat situation she'd stumbled into than the trauma to Blood. She'd dealt with trauma before, despite being only twenty. She'd done her nursing school right out of high school and had opted for the associates program, so she'd done it in two years. While in school, she'd worked for Argent in their company hospital. That alone hadn't prepared her for this kind of trauma, but they'd had her working in field hospitals all over the world in war-torn areas, though always far away from the fighting. She still got to see the wounds, but had been sheltered from combat.

She sat carefully in a nearby seat, not wanting to draw attention to herself. No one looked at her, but talked in clusters amongst themselves. She just wanted a drink of water.

As if reading her mind, the big African-American man who'd helped her get Blood to safety loomed over her with a small smile, handing her a bottle of water.

"You look like you could use it."

"Thanks," she said softly.

"I'm Shadow," he said, introducing himself. "My buddy there is Trucker." The other man, the one who'd driven them here, grinned at her.

"Alizay. Everyone calls me Ali." When they both offered her their hand, she shook them. "Lucky you had that box in the back."

"Yeah." Trucker scrubbed his hand through his hair. "Snagged it on the way out in case I needed to store extra ammo. Not really sure why I grabbed it instead of one of the plastic tubs. Guess I figured the cardboard would be easier to get rid of if we needed the space. Good idea, by the way."

"It wasn't my idea. That's just an easy way to move someone with a pelvic injury without causing too much more damage or pain."

"You a medic?" Shadow had a congenial smile on his face but there was no mistaking the fact he was going to interrogate her.

"Nurse. I work here at Argent."

"Argent also lets me contract her out on occasion." The big man walking toward them looked familiar, but she couldn't place him.

"I'm Joe Gill. Owner of ExFil. Alex let me borrow you a few times when you were in school. Bet he's glad he did now."

"I'm glad he did," she said, extending her hand to him. "Ali."

"Everyone calls me Cain, Ali."

"Thorn," Cain called over his shoulder. "Got someone you need to meet."

Alizay wished he hadn't called attention to her. She hated being the center of things.

"This the young woman who saved Blood's ass?"

"It is. Ali, this is Thorn. He's the president of Salvation's Bane. I'm president of Bones. Do you know what we are?"

Alizay stilled. "So, the rumors are true. ExFil is owned by bikers."

Cain grinned. "It is. We live by our own codes. I guess you could say it's our way of staying sane outside of the service." He nodded at men behind Thorn. "These assholes are Beast and Vicious. Don't let the names fool you, they're basically harmless."

"Now, why don't I believe that?" Alizay was getting more and more nervous. She had the feeling something shady was going on but had no idea what to do about it.

Thorn laughed. "Because you're fuckin' smart. Look. Cain said you've worked with ExFil before."

"Yeah. But I just now figured out it was ExFil that sent me. I thought it was Argent. They paid for my school, and I worked for them while I was going, but I had no idea Argent had rented me out."

"You know you were never in any danger. Right?" Cain said softly. "I made sure you were protected all the time. Alex said you needed experience with trauma but wanted you protected. I did, too. Don't like sending out young women with no military training into those types of situations. I always had you covered."

"Oh. No. I didn't know that. I was just glad to get the experience. Mr. Petrov and Mr. Ivanovich explained the risks to me before I went and said that I could refuse if I was uncomfortable."

"Bastards," Vicious muttered. "They should have made it clear you were safe and who to go to if you didn't feel safe."

"They wanted me to work through my fear," she said softly. "I'm not a very adventurous person."

"Well, you proved yourself today," Thorn said. "In spades."

"I can smell flattery a mile away, Mr. Thorn. You want something."

Thorn had the good grace to look sheepish, scrubbing the back of his neck with his hand. "I've asked for your services through Argent again. Cain agreed."

Alizay stood, straightening and putting her shoulders back. She was proud of her abilities. If they needed her to go into a hostile area to help their wounded, she was more than willing. "What's my job?"

Thorn pointed casually in the general of the surgical suite where Blood was currently being put back together. "He's gonna need help when he gets out of this. Alex said you were the perfect person for the job. You willin'?"

She blinked. That wasn't what she'd been expecting at all. While she preferred the kind of work Thorn was suggesting -- taking care of a patient and helping them get better each day -- she wasn't sure about this particular job.

"I have the feeling it would be even more challenging than field nursing. That man in there isn't going to be a good patient. He's not the kind of man to do what he's supposed to in order to heal properly. He's going to push himself past the point that's good for him. Anyone can see that just by the way he held himself together after he was injured."

"Did I mention you were fuckin' smart?" Thorn said with a big smile.

"Flattery..."

"Yeah, well, I'm willin' to use everything I can to get you to agree to this. If it's money, you don't have to worry about it. I'll compensate you nicely."

"Yet another tick in the 'no' column. The more you're willing to pay, the less you want to deal with him yourself."

They all chuckled at Thorn's expense. "You sound just like my ol' lady," Thorn grumbled, but Ali could see the grin tugging at his lips. "Come on. He's hurt. He needs your delicate, feminine touch."

"Before I agree to this, I want to see what he's like when he wakes up. How much he bitches and moans will determine how willing I am to take this on. I have to tell you, I can't say there's much of a chance of convincing me he would accept my help."

Thorn winced. "Fuck." He exchanged a look with Cain, who simply shrugged. "Got nothin' to lose." He stuck out his hand to Alizay. "We'll give it a try when he's awake."

Chapter Three

Pain was a real thing, though Blood couldn't seem to claw his way through the haze fogging his mind. His leg hurt like a motherfucker, but he could feel his toes moving against something when he tried to move. That had to be a good thing. Right?

He remembered the blast in the street, knocking him off his feet. He thought his leg got caught as another blast rocked him, and that was when he'd been hurt. Not when the concussion had hit him or when he'd been caught at the edge of the first blast, though he must have. He even thought he remembered his brothers coming through the explosions unharmed, or, at least, not hurt as badly as they should have been. Perhaps that fucking thin-ass armor Alex had forced on them had worked. That was when he remembered Shadow being unable to get the armor off him.

And the girl who had finally done it.

Dreaming. He had to have been dreaming. No woman looked like that. She was like his own personal angel. All golden hair and gloriously blue eyes. She'd freed him and seen to his injury. Then he'd passed out. But he remembered her name.

Alizay.

She'd smiled and the whole world had narrowed to her lovely face. At least, that was how he remembered it. He could almost feel her soft hand in his right now.

"Blood…"

Ah, God. He was hallucinating. He could still hear her calling his name. Except she didn't know his name. Did she? He tried to speak, but his mouth felt like it was stuffed full of cotton. He tried to shift toward her voice, but the moment he did, pain shot through his hip and pelvis with such agony he knew he cried out.

"Easy, there. Let me help."

Gentle hands maneuvered him so that his weight shifted back off his hip. Then there was a warm sensation going up his arm and the pain faded. Along with everything else...

* * *

The next time he woke, there was a blonde head lying on the bed beside him. He didn't see any blood, so he assumed there was a body attached to it and, really, why was that his first thought anyway? Long, silvery-golden locks fanned out, covering her elbow where she'd bent it to use her arm as a pillow. It was impossible not to pick up a thick lock and let it slide through his fingers. It felt so good against his skin he did it again. Then wrapped the lock around his finger a couple of times.

"Wha --?" She started a little, but lifted her head slowly to look at him. "Blood," she sighed. His name on her lips made his cock stir even though his body was battered as fuck. When the sleep slowly cleared from her eyes, she gave him a gentle smile. "I'm sorry. Must have fallen asleep."

"Time is it?" His words were still slurred, and he still couldn't focus his thoughts well, but he knew the woman looking at him was the most beautiful thing he'd ever seen. No way there were two angels in his life. This had to be the same woman from the street.

She blinked a couple of times, then sat up, her hair sifting through his fingers like the softest silk. Scrubbing her hands over her face, she groaned once then looked at her watch. "'Bout two in the morning. You in pain?"

"No." He was, but he didn't want more meds. Not yet. "Who are you?"

She sighed, stretching. Blood noticed her wince and rub her neck. "I'm Alizay. I helped get your body armor off. Your team had me stay with you until we got you to the hospital."

"Well, I'm obviously in the hospital," he groaned, trying to shift his weight himself. The pain was sharp and cutting, but he managed to stave off more than a small wince. "Yet you're still here."

She sat up straighter, blinking rapidly as if he'd struck her. Then she shrugged. "Your people think you need a babysitter while you're getting well."

"Babysitter?"

"Yeah. Something about you not being capable of lying still so you can heal properly." She crossed her arms. It should have looked like she was putting her stubborn on, but instead, she looked like she was drawing in on herself. Like he'd somehow hurt her. Probably with his gruff tone. "But nothing's set in stone. I'm just here for a trial. If you really don't want me with you or I decide you're just not worth the effort, I'll be on my way, and you'll be able to do what you want, when you want." She grinned at him, but it didn't quite make it to her eyes. This deal was far from done.

"Don't need no damned babysitter. But I might be able to use a nurse." Blood tried to make it sound lascivious, but the pain was starting to cut into him. To him, he sounded too much like he *did* need a nurse.

"You might. I get the feeling you don't want one though."

"Not sure why you'd think that. You put on one of those little hats, the short dress and thigh-high stockings, and I'll feel much, much better."

"Right. Not happening."

"You don't fraternize with the patients?" He gave her what he hoped was a cocky grin.

"Nope. I don't own stockings, can't work in a dress, and I burned the little hat after graduation."

Blood barked out a laugh that sent pain radiating through his lower body with each movement. The second he grimaced, she was up and by his side. She looked at the machine at the bedside. He noticed it was connected to a tube pumping fluid into his arm. She looked at the readout and picked up the button laying at his side.

"This is your pain pump delivery. You're allowed a certain amount every hour in addition to what it delivers regularly." Before he could tell her he didn't need that shit, she firmly pressed the button. "I know you were going to say you don't need it, but you do. The more you sleep right now the better. In a couple of days, they'll take you off it slowly. With you fresh out of a major surgery, right now you need to stay on top of the pain or you'll just be miserable."

"You shoulda given me a chance to refuse it."

"I'll remember that in the future. Won't change my actions. If I think you need something, I'm doing it regardless of what you want. When you're well enough to stop me, you can."

"Little witch," he muttered.

"Noted." She didn't smile at him, but she did brush a lock of hair off his forehead gently. "Just let it help you sleep. Then you can get better and do what you want."

"Don't think I won't," he said, his words slurring again. "Keepin' track of every time you pull rank, too. Spankin' you for it." Then he passed out.

* * *

"Where's my motherfuckin' keys!"

The bellow wasn't lost on anyone in the vicinity if the way everyone scattered was any indication. Except Alizay. Blood was on what Alizay had called "driving probation." Why she thought he wasn't fit enough to drive or ride his bike was beyond him. So what if he had trouble standing when he first got up? So what if they'd stuck him in a wheelchair? It had only been a week since the accident. He was allowed to be a little slow from time to time and didn't really need assistance. His body would adjust. The doc said he had replaced his right femur and hip joint. So far, he'd avoided the rehab bit. No way he was doing a bunch of needless, repetitive shit. He was strong. Fit. He could do this on his own.

"Keys? What keys?" That voice. Fucking woman had a voice like sin. Didn't mean he'd give in to her demands on the fucking rehab.

"You know fuckin' well what keys! I want the keys to my bike!"

"I'm so sorry, Blood," she said with a sweet, innocent lilt that nearly had him believing she *was* sweet and innocent. "Last time I used them I'm pretty sure I hung them on the key rack by the door in your room."

"There is no fuckin' key rack in my room, you little witch!"

Alizay had the nerve to look at him with those big, blue eyes all wide and guileless and straight up lying to him. "Goodness gracious me! I coulda swore that's where I put them. Are you sure you don't have a key rack?"

"Woman…"

"I'm sure if we work together we can find them. I mean, I don't know your people that well, so maybe I gave them to the wrong person?"

"You know damned well exactly where you put them!"

Which he knew without a doubt was accurate. She'd probably put them in the gym. The one place Blood had been avoiding the three days he'd been out of the hospital and in the big mansion the men from Shadow Demons pretended to call a clubhouse. The one place he knew his brothers and the physical therapists were lying in wait to ambush him. Blood knew the plan. If everyone just happened to be in the gym when she took the keys in, and just happened to hear her say they had one shot at this, that she was putting the keys on the other side of the room and they'd better make sure they had the door locked... well. Yeah. Blood knew what the little vixen was about. He had his ways.

"Where was the last place you had them?" She gave him what had to be her most innocent, wide-eyed look. Just a girl trying to be helpful. He just stared at her. So, she tried again. "I bet if you backtracked your steps, you could find them."

He waited a few beats of silence, giving her that death stare, before answering. "I can't retrace my steps because I've not been stepping. I've been in a fuckin' wheelchair for three fuckin' days. I want to ride my fuckin' bike. Now where are my fuckin' keys?" He basically roared the question at her. Alizay didn't back down. Which, Blood could say might have turned him on. Just a little bit.

"When you calm down and decide you want to ask nicely for my help in finding your keys, you can find me in the gym. If I'm not going to be helping you with your rehab, then I'll get in a good workout myself."

Oh, she was good...

Blood watched as she turned and walked down the hall, her tight little ass swaying side to side in those insanely tight yoga pants. Why did women always seem to wear those things? And this woman knew how to wear them. She was obviously very fit, if slight of build. As he watched, she stripped off her T-shirt, leaving her in a strappy sports bra. She didn't look over her shoulder to see if he watched. Just continued on down the hall, ass swaying as she did. Then she pushed open the door to the gym and slipped inside.

Before he realized it, Blood found himself following her. Using a cane, damn it, not the wheelchair. He hated that he had to use assistance to get where he was going. It was embarrassing, but the truth was he needed it. Maybe the rehab wouldn't be a bad thing. Especially if he got to ogle little nurse Alizay's body.

The second he stepped into the big room, Blood knew he was in trouble. Every member of Salvation's Bane still in the compound was there. A few had gone back to Palm Springs, but Carnage, Stryker, Tobias, and, strangely, Shadow from Bones, had stayed behind.

"Glad you could join us, brother," Carnage greeted him. "Wondered how long it would take you to finally give in and do as the doctor ordered."

"Fuck all y'all. OK?"

"Hey, just tryin' to help a brother out." Tobias grinned. He also gave Alizay a sidelong glance. "Gotta tell ya. Ain't never seen no rehab facility with this kinda view." All his brothers looked at the small figure currently running on the treadmill, her back to them all. Her ass was a work of art. There was just the slightest bit of jiggle to it as she moved. Her back was mostly bare. The sports bra she wore covered her small breasts, but the back was a series of straps that revealed skin all over the damned place. Alizay was definitely fit. Not overly muscled, but sinewy and firm all over.

"Don't need you guys in here making it more difficult than it already is," he said, trying his best not to growl at them ogling nurse Alizay. "Besides, she's a fucking kid."

"She's twenty. That's legal no matter who you are." Shadow grinned at him lasciviously. "Gotta tell you, if I were you, I'd be all over my therapy like stink on shit."

"Don't need no therapy. I'll get through this like I always do. Didn't do therapy after Afghanistan. Don't need it now."

"Well, Thorn says otherwise," Carnage said.

"Cain agrees." Shadow shook his head and crossed his arms over his chest. "You're on leave until you complete your rehab. Said if that meant you spent Christmas here, so be it. And you know how the women are about Christmas. If we all have to stay here with you, they'll be invading this place in force."

"Also," Carnage added with a grin. "I've heard that Suzie has made a friend here. Name's Bellarose. 'Bout the same age. Girl has a wicked sense of humor and will catch you unawares with the red glitter for your beard." He tilted his head sideways, obviously looking at Blood's beard. "With all that white, you could almost pass for a Santa. Just need to cover the tats everywhere else."

"You've got to be fuckin' kiddin' me." Blood wanted to lash out, but his attention was focused on the sweet ass gently bouncing on the treadmill a few feet away.

"Nope. In fact, you're not even allowed back into the clubhouse until your doctor is satisfied with your progress." Stryker's grin was almost enough for his brother to earn himself a fist to the face, but Blood had other things to worry about. Like what those tight little yoga pants would look like on Alizay from the front...

"Fine. But I ain't havin' an audience. If I'm doin' this, it's gonna be on my own terms, my own way."

"Fine," Shadow said. "As long as the doc and your therapist pass you, don't matter how you do it. He did your first exam after surgery yesterday. You've got one month before they eval you again. You don't show significant improvement by then, Cain says he's steppin' in. That don't work, he's suspending you indefinitely."

Blood leveled his gaze on Shadow. "You can tell Cain to kiss my ass. I did my job. He don't like the way I do things now, he can take a flying leap."

"You know he's more concerned about you than anything else, Blood. He's trying to motivate you."

"He's threatenin' me." Blood looked at all his brothers. He wasn't really angry with them, he was just lashing out because it was the only way he could release some of this emotion building inside him. He could already tell he was never going to have the range of movement he was used to again. He'd been down this road before. Rebuilt limbs were never as good as real ones. "Don't take well to threats. So you can all kiss my whole entire ass."

"Good," Tobias said, slapping his riding gloves over his thigh. He'd rested his foot on a nearby chair. "But I'm not licking the fuckin' hole. Just get on your therapist... er... therapy. The sooner you get to it the better you're gonna be."

The brothers roared. Blood just flipped them off.

Chapter Four

Yeah. Alizay had heard the entire conversation. She only hoped they'd take her red face and neck as being from exertion, not embarrassment. They might think she was nothing more than a fuck toy, but she was very good at her job. And she was a consummate professional. In retrospect, perhaps she should have worn sweats and a long T-shirt, but this was how she always dressed to work out. When she was working closely with Blood, she decided she'd put on a T-shirt. That would make matters easier. Although her sports bra was stylish, and covered everything -- not even cleavage showed -- it was still a bra. Sure, the guys they were all shirtless, but knowing they were watching made her self-conscious.

Alizay had been around fit, deadly men her entire adult life. None of them could compare to any one of the men from Salvation's Bane or Bones. She was beginning to realize she might be in a little bit of trouble because she had images of every one of them, flexing shirtless, running on endless loops in her mind. And yeah. She'd seem them flexing. Goofing off in the gym, but eye candy galore.

Now she was faced with the most brooding one of the bunch. She had the feeling that, if Blood weren't injured, he'd be pleasant to be around. So far, he was proving to be her worst patient ever.

She heard the rest of his posse leaving and kind of hoped he'd left with them. She hadn't been lying. Exactly. His keys had been in the gym. Currently, she thought Tobias had them. But it could have been Carnage. Her job had been to get him into the gym. Their job had been to keep him there. So far he hadn't left, but Alizay didn't have hopes of him staying much longer.

"So, I'm here," he said, sidling up next to the treadmill. "Give me your best shot, little Ali."

Alizay slowed the treadmill until it stopped gradually. She snagged the towel she'd hung over the handrail in front of her and blotted the sweat from her skin. It was more to give herself time to compose herself. Blood was a potent man. The way he looked at her was like he was looking into her soul. She couldn't help but recall his words in the hospital when he'd told her he was "keepin' track of every time you pull rank," and "spankin' you for it." He'd been half delirious with pain and narcotics, but Alizay knew he'd meant every word, and that he'd remember the promise.

"How serious are you about this?" she asked. "Because I'm here at Mr. Petrov's request. If you have no intention of following my instructions, then I'm not wasting my time on you."

Blood shrugged. "I'll do whatever you tell me to. Ain't like it's a big deal, even if I can do all this shit on my own."

"I take it you've been injured before? Gone through rehab?"

"Other hip. Ain't never worked right. Don't expect this one to either."

"Did you take to that therapy with the gusto you're showing with me? Because if you don't really commit yourself, you're never going to get strong again."

"Just get on with it," he snapped, reaching the end of his patience. "What do we do first?"

So Alizay took him through the first steps. She measured his range of motion, his strength, his pain. Then started working him on strength-building for the surrounding muscles. Core strength. Back strength. All of which she insisted were necessary for when they started the real work. Three times a week. The other days he'd spend on the treadmill for his therapy time. They'd work out for longer intervals as they progressed. More than once, he referred to her as "Nurse Ratchet."

Alizay didn't want to push him too hard, but wanted him to get the feeling he was being pushed. It was important for him to feel like he was just out of reach of his goal. It hadn't taken long for her to figure out Blood had the type of personality that wouldn't let him fail. If he was one rep away from meeting his goal, he would push just that little bit past what everyone thought he could do to finish.

She worked him two hours. By the end, he was sweating and grimacing more than she'd have liked, so she called the doc and got some pain meds on the way.

"Stop," she said when he continued with the resistance band, working his quadriceps. "Hydrate." After two hours of dealing with the prickly, dominant man, she was past niceties.

"I'm not done yet." He gritted his teeth together, obviously focusing on the last few reps he had. Alizay was having none of it.

"You're done when I say you're done." She took her trauma shears and cut the band in two so it snapped away from his foot. "You're done." For emphasis, she tossed a water bottle at him. "Drink the whole thing, then hit the showers." She pushed a wheelchair close to where he sat, not suggesting he use it. Not *not* suggesting it either.

"Get that fuckin' thing away from me, girl! Ain't usin' it."

"You fall, you risk damaging that leg even worse than it is." She gave him her sternest look. "If you don't use it, at least use the cane."

"Ain't using either."

"You're being ridiculous. No one's going to see you, and you need to be careful right after an aggressive workout. I can see this is probably where you failed the last time."

Without warning, Blood exploded to his feet and took two menacing steps toward her. The third step was on his weak leg, and it just crumpled. Thankfully, Alizay was on her guard and hadn't backed off when he looked like he was going to threaten her. She dove for him, catching him around the waist from the front. When they went down, Alizay twisted so she took the brunt of the fall, cushioning Blood to minimize the jarring of his leg. But he landed squarely on top of her. Heavily.

Finally, Blood rolled them over. Alizay sprawled on top of him, the wind knocked out of her.

"You good?" His voice was gruff and laced with pain. His arms were around her tightly.

"I-I don't know. Give me a second."

"Take all the time you need, sugar." His arms tightened just a fraction and he sighed, laying back on the mat, his breath more than a little bit ragged.

Wow. Holy shit! Yeah, she needed to get up. Those arms wrapped around her seemed to swallow her whole, and Alizay loved the feel of his body against hers. She had to pull herself together. He was her patient, not a gigolo, for crying out loud. But, God, it felt so good! She'd never been in this position before. When she was overseas learning how to be a trauma nurse, she'd been strictly off limits to the guys there. It had been thoroughly explained to her from the very beginning. She'd been instructed to keep her hands to herself as much as the guys had. It had been fine by her then. Now, however, she realized how much she was missing out on.

Finally, she found her breath and footing. Pushing up, she held out her hand to him. He scowled at her, pushing himself up and snagging the cane instead of taking her hand. Then, surprisingly, he lowered himself into the chair and shoved off toward the showers without another word.

* * *

What the fuck had just happened? Blood couldn't quite wrap his mind around the incident that had just played out. One second he was about to throttle Alizay -- not really, but he'd wanted to make an impression. The next, he'd been falling. She'd thrown herself at him, wrapping her body around him enough that she'd padded his fall. He was the man in this situation, for crying out loud. If anyone was protecting someone it should be him protecting her. Yet, he'd quite probably hurt her by letting her take the brunt of it. He'd known Alizay had had the breath knocked out of her, but he could have really hurt her. He had to be twice her weight. What if she'd broken a rib?

Fuck!

Normally, Blood couldn't have given a fuck, but he didn't intentionally hurt women. If he had to kill, he did it humanely. This was different. He'd needlessly put her in harm's way because of his stubbornness.

Now he sat naked in the chair, washing the sweat from his body. Lesson learned there. He'd use the chair or the cane until he was stronger. It had only been a few days since he'd woken from the surgery. He'd actually been out of it for two days immediately afterward. It had been another couple of days before he'd been cleared to start his rehab. Blood had fought it from the beginning and, had it not been for this little mishap, he'd still be fighting it. He was a fucking Green Beret, for crying out loud! He didn't need fucking rehab.

Except maybe Alizay had a point. He was always the first person to tell his men to ask for help. Better to ask for help than fuck things up. And he'd royally fucked things up.

"You OK?" Alizay's voice came from the big walk-in shower's entrance. Of course she'd follow him in there.

Blood winced. The water hit his bare skin, the soap sluicing off him to the chair before finally sliding down the drain. "Fine. I promise I won't get out of the chair while I'm in here. I'll be fine."

"I know," she said. He could hear her stepping inside. It was a group shower, designed like any gym shower. No privacy, multiple shower heads, and wide-open spaces for maneuvering wheelchairs and other equipment around with ease. "I need to make sure you didn't hurt your leg."

"I didn't. You took the brunt of the fall." Blood clenched his fists. "Next time, you let me fuckin' fall."

"You know I can't do that," she said softly. Blood heard her footfalls on the tile and knew she was barefooted. "I have to check your incisions."

He looked back at her over his shoulder. "You know I'm naked. Right? I only say that because I'm not apologizin' for any reaction I have to you bein' all wet in here with me."

Blood felt a surge of satisfaction as color crept up Alizay's neck and into her face. God, she was lovely. Pale blonde hair, alabaster skin. And that sleek, tight body… He'd love to strip her bare and pull her into his lap right now. He might be in a wheelchair at the moment, but he'd bet he could still give her a good seeing to. What would his little Nurse Ratchet look like in the throes of passion? Oh yeah, he'd love to see that.

Deciding he'd push her a little, he reached for the four-pronged cane she'd originally hooked over the back of his chair and stood. He turned to face her, his cock semi hard and rapidly getting harder.

Alizay swallowed, her gaze latching onto it before skittering away. "Uh, turn around," she said. He could see her whole body trembling where she stood. She was barefoot, but still dressed in her workout clothes. Water splashed over her legs, wetting the stretchy material, and beaded on her stomach. What he wouldn't give to trace a few of those drops of water over her muscled abdomen? He'd use his lips and tongue. And, yeah. He had no doubt she'd be delicious.

Blood did as she instructed and turned to face away from her. Soon after, soft, gentle fingers traced the skin beside his incision before probing a little deeper, probably examining the joint as best she could.

"Hurt?"

"Aches," he said, not meaning his hip.

"I have some pain meds ready for you. If you need more, I can ask the doc."

"Honey, what I need, the doc can't provide." He looked back at her again, a cocky smile firmly in place. "Well, he could, but I don't swing that way."

She gasped, standing abruptly. "I… that's not appropriate."

Blood shrugged. "Appropriate or not, you're a good-lookin' woman. Besides, I've got the feelin' you're not as immune to me as you'd like me to think."

* * *

Sweet God, he was right. Alizay was more attracted to Blood than any man she'd ever seen. Sure, he was abrasive at best, a complete asshole at times, but she knew it was the force of his personality and being so badly injured and at the mercy of his battered body. He was a man who had to be in control. This situation was exactly the kind of thing that would make him super grumpy.

Didn't mean she couldn't see the caring side of him. He was angry that she'd broken his fall, not because it showed weakness on his part but because he felt like he should be the one taking care of her. She knew it like she knew her own name. She'd seen it many times when strong alpha males got hurt. They hated having the little woman taking care of them. Blood was no different in that regard. What was different was her reaction to him versus her reaction to any other man she'd helped during her admittedly short career.

She'd seen men as fit as Blood naked before. She might technically be a virgin, but she'd seen -- and felt -- her share of naked men. Just not in a sexual situation. No matter who it was or what the situation happened to be, she'd never once thought about sex with a patient. Now, she was going to have a very hard time not thinking about sex with Blood. Looking into his eyes now, Blood saw her attraction and would most likely do everything he could to capitalize on it.

She finished her examination, then urged him to sit back in the chair. "Doesn't seem like you hurt anything too badly. I'll leave you to finish." She started to turn, then added, "I'm sorry."

He raised an eyebrow at her. "For what?"

"For upsetting you enough to come after me on a less-than-sound leg." She gestured around her. "And for invading your privacy. I just didn't want you in here by yourself if you were hurt. I'll get someone else next time."

His hand reached out and snagged her wrist. "First of all, I was being an ass. Ain't gonna lie. Being sidelined is a bitch, and I've been taking out my frustration on you. Second, I'm your patient. You wouldn't want your boss to think you weren't doing your job, would you?"

Alizay answered without hesitation. "I wouldn't want my boss to think I was encouraging my patient to flirt with me. It's highly frowned upon."

"You let me worry about that. You're my nurse and my therapist. You take care of me." He gave her a sly smile. "In fact, I may have to insist you never leave my side until my therapy is deemed a success."

She gasped. "You know that could take months. You're not going to be here that long, and I can't leave when you do."

"Who says I won't be here that long? Cain says I'm here until Doc says I can go. If I'm doin' this fuckin' therapy, I'm doin' it someplace with the best equipment and the best people. And yeah. If I leave, you're leaving with me." He made the declaration with the air of a man who knew he could pull it off.

"I'm not leaving my family."

He narrowed his eyes at her. "You married? Got a man?"

If she were smart, Alizay knew she should lie. It was on the tip of her tongue to do exactly that then her mouth betrayed her. "No. But the people here are the only family I have. I'm not leaving them."

Blood grinned. And the effect was devastating. "Yeah. You'll go with me wherever I go. I'll make sure Alex gets the memo." He grinned, then turned the chair around so he faced her directly. "If you wouldn't mind handing me a towel?" Obediently, she did. "Now," he said as he absently toweled himself off. "My clothes are in the locker room. I could use some help getting dressed."

"Seriously? You go from practically shoving me out the door to wanting me to help you get dressed?"

"Well, you pointed out I'm not at a hundred percent yet. I don't want to accidentally hurt myself worse by overdoing it. And you did push me pretty hard earlier. My leg's tired." The expression on Blood's face was a cross between a pouting child and one who'd just found the motherlode of candy stashed in his Christmas stocking.

Had she not felt so bad about him falling, knowing she'd practically goaded him into his tantrum, Alizay might have told him to fuck off. Instead, she sighed and pushed him into the locker room and did exactly as he asked.

Lord help her if he kept this up…

Chapter Five

Three months later...

Blood had thrown himself into the fucking rehab and had refused to let Alex call in another therapist when Alizay said she he was ready to move on. Though he'd taken to goading and tormenting Alizay, he'd insisted they not replace her. On more than one occasion, she'd thrown things at him, usually something soft, but once she'd chucked a two-pound dumbbell his way. Every time he vexed her, she pushed him harder. Which was what he wanted to begin with. He just had to make her mad enough to give him what he needed. He'd also resigned himself to spending Christmas and New Year's at the Shadow Demon compound. But, honestly, gourmet meals and high-tech facilities were no hardship whatsoever.

"You know, you could just tell her you wanted a more vigorous routine," Alex Petrov said with an amused look. "She might respond better."

"Now... what fun... would that be?" Blood was currently doing one-legged squats, pushing his hips and thigh as hard as he could. Sweat streamed down his face with his effort and his sentence came out broken as he sucked in lungfuls of air. "Besides... I tried that. She wasn't... on board."

"You know, she's got access to lethal doses of morphine. You might want to reconsider your behavior."

Blood paused and grinned at the leader of the Shadow Demons. "Anything worth having is worth a little pain to get it."

"Yeah, but is it worth your life?"

Starting up again, Blood nodded, grinning broadly. "Oh, yeah. Definitely."

"You're supposed to be working! Not talking!"

Speak of the devil. The woman in question stormed across the mat to him. "How am I supposed to meet the ridiculously high goals you set with the doc if you don't do what I tell you?"

Technically, Blood was doing far more, but he liked to make her think he wasn't doing as well as he was. In fact, he felt like he would be in the best shape of his life after this. He continually complained to the doc that she wasn't pushing him hard enough, so he knew the doc gave her shit. He also knew the doc was fully aware of his real progress and liked to push Alizay's boundaries from time to time same as Blood did. Said it kept her honest. Blood decided that, while he enjoyed goading her and having help doing it, he might have to punch the doc in the face for picking on his woman when this was all over. And yeah. He was man enough to admit he wanted little Alizay, aka Nurse Ratchet, all to himself.

He waved Alex away as he stopped and gave Alizay a lopsided grin. "Maybe if you took a more… hands-on approach."

There it was. The second the words penetrated her brain, the sexual innuendo sent heat creeping up her neck and into her face. Blood loved making her blush like that. It was almost as if the woman had never been flirted with before. Sure, she'd said she didn't flirt with patients, but Blood thought there was more to it.

"I'll just leave you two alone," Alex said, giving Alizay a two-finger salute as he turned and left the gym.

"If you get me fired, Blood, I'll cut off your balls!"

"Hmm… how about instead you just suck them? That could be fun."

"Asshole!" She tossed a wadded-up towel at him.

Blood laughed as he snagged it out of the air, wiping the sweat off his face. "You could lick my asshole if you wanted. Sure." When she sputtered angrily at him, he raised his hands as if in surrender. "All right, all right. You don't have to do that. I'll lick yours instead. You know. Right before I fuck it. That could be really fun."

With a screech, Alizay launched herself at him full force. Had he truly been as unsteady on his feet as he'd made her believe, he'd probably have fallen on his ass, but he caught her in midair, wrapping his arms tightly around her, pulling her tiny, compact body against his and holding her securely.

"You bastard! You've been goldbricking!"

He chuckled. "Maybe. You saying you intended to knock me on my ass? That wouldn't be very nice, now would it?"

"You deserve it!"

"What if you'd hurt my hip? Coulda snapped the hardware." He was just being a bastard now, but, again, he couldn't help himself.

"You're standing on three layers of mats. No way there could have been that much force."

"Just think about how horribly you'd have felt if it had, though." Blood didn't let her go as he sank to his knees on the mat. Instead, he urged her legs around his waist. She let him, doing exactly what he wanted. Once on his knees, he held her to him with one arm while he used the other arm to catch himself as he eased her down so she lay on her back on the mat. Blood stretched out above her, pulling her more securely against him as he settled himself. "I'd be lying here in tremendous pain. You'd be on top of me, afraid to move because it would hurt me worse." He shook his head as he lowered his face to hers. "You might have had to kiss it and make it better."

Before she could reply, Blood settled his mouth on hers. Moving his lips over hers was the most erotic thing Blood had ever imagined. She whimpered beneath him, her body stiffening, then melting, then stiffening again. It was as if she had no idea what to do. Blood knew the feeling. He didn't know whether to continue kissing her or to strip her naked and feast on every gloriously bare inch of her body.

He lapped at her, nipping her bottom lip slightly until she gasped, giving him entry. God, she tasted sweet! Blood slid his tongue inside her mouth, licking the inside of her cheeks and the roof of her mouth before tangling her tongue with his. She moaned into his mouth, arching her neck, reaching for him as she whimpered.

"That's it, sweetness. Let me kiss you."

"I -- B-Blood…" Alizay's sighs were soft and content yet made him believe she was anxious for more. He could almost imagine she wanted him as much as he wanted her. Hell, maybe she did. He also knew she'd never admit it under normal circumstances. Which meant he had to take what she'd let him right now and convince her to give him the rest later.

* * *

The vast array of equipment in the gym was eerily silent. There was a faint sound of a door opening and closing off in the distance. Probably Alex exiting the gym. If she were lucky. The problem was, it wouldn't have mattered if fifty people had filed through that door. Alizay was focused on nothing other than the sensations Blood had created throughout her with just a kiss.

His teeth and tongue mastered her. She was putty in his hands, and there was nothing she could do about it. Alizay wasn't sure she even wanted to do anything about it. The sensations he created in her were like nothing she'd ever known. Never had sex been anything more than a means to an end. It was a manipulation tool at best, a power struggle at worst.

But what Blood made her feel... Fiction could never do this justice. His skin moving against hers was more than lust or desire. It was... an awakening. As if her whole life to this point had been just about living. Surviving. Now there was this other avenue of life she was eager to explore. But only with Blood. Maybe there could have been other men she was attracted to if they'd only kissed her first, but Alizay knew in her heart this was the one. Blood would be the man she'd forever compare any other man to.

And it freaked her out.

She couldn't stop the whimper that escaped her, or a feeble attempt to push him away. She needed Blood to stop, yet couldn't bear the thought of not feeling his lips on her body. The second she stiffened, he growled and wrapped his arms around her tighter.

"Stop thinking, Alizay. Just feel." The words were rasped at her ear just before he took the lobe between his lips and sucked. "Listen. Listen to your body."

"I can't --"

"Why not?" Blood nipped her neck before laving away the hurt with the flat of his tongue on the way back to her ear. "Why not just enjoy the moment? I can make you feel good, and I think you know it."

"But my job…"

"Is perfectly safe. You think Alex doesn't know what I want? He knows. If he'd objected, he would have warned me off and he wouldn't have left us alone because he knows I'm capable of getting what I want."

"Oh, God," she whimpered before he took her mouth again.

How was she supposed to resist this? The very thought that Mr. Petrov knew what they were doing sent a surge of panic through her. She should be fighting Blood. Fighting her own very real attraction to him.

But before she could process anything more, or act on what she knew she should do, Alizay had wrapped her arms around Blood's neck and her legs around his waist. She not only let him kiss her, but she kissed him back just as passionately. It must have been exactly what Blood wanted, because he grunted once before sliding her more firmly against him and deepening the kiss.

When Blood rested his full weight on her, rocking against her so that his cock slid up and down between her legs, Alizay gave a sharp cry. Her limbs tightened even more around him, her heels digging into his ass.

"That's it, baby," he praised her. "You like me touchin' you. Don't you?"

She didn't answer, but she really didn't need to. It was pretty obvious given the noise she was making as well as the way she clung to him. And the way she moved her body against his. There was no doubt she'd be embarrassed once this was over.

"Oh, no, baby. You don't get to think about this," he purred. "Close your eyes." His lips trailed over her neck, his hands gripping her hips. Those big palms closed around her like a cage. "Feel my lips on your skin." It wasn't long before she did. Just below her bra, Blood's mouth brushed over her belly, moving ever lower. Sometimes he kissed, sometimes he nipped. When he licked, she let out a sharp cry, arching her back.

But when he chuckled at her reaction, it was like he'd dumped a bucket of icy water over her.

"No!" Alizay twisted her body out of his grasp, crawling across the mat away from him. She absolutely had to put space between herself and Blood if she wanted to keep her self-respect. She'd fallen down that stupid rabbit hole once again, and this time she was very much afraid she'd never find her way out again. "Stay away!" Though she was several feet away from him, Alizay still crab-walked backward until she sat with her back against the wall. Slowly, she stood, readying herself to bolt if he tried to keep her with him.

"Easy, girl." Blood stood slowly, keeping his hands out in a non-threatening gesture. "I ain't gonna jump on you."

"Oh yeah? What do you call that?" she yelled at him, more angry with herself than Blood.

To her surprise, he just chuckled. "Sorry, darlin', but that was all you. I was an innocent bystander in all this." He winked at her. "Well, mostly. But I was just following your lead."

That made it even worse. Because he was a hundred percent right. She'd launched herself at him, trying to tackle him to the mat in a fit of anger. If he saw her now as nothing more than another woman in his club, throwing herself at whichever biker she wanted that week, how could she really be angry with him? This situation was entirely her fault. She'd promised herself *never again*. She absolutely would not put herself in this kind of situation again. Yet here she was. Letting a man use her body for his own purpose. Blood wanted out of his therapy? What better way to get what he wanted than by seducing the therapist? Problem was, this time, she had no idea what she was getting out of it, other than a broken heart. Because she might actually feel something for the jackass.

"I know," she whispered. Then she cleared her throat and put her shoulders back. She still couldn't look at him. "Now, if you'll excuse me, I need a sh--" she cleared her throat. "I, uh, need to, uh, head back to, uh… I'm going to my room." She practically fled from the gym like hell was on her heels. Because like it or not, she might have inadvertently started something she had no hope of finishing. Definitely not if she expected to keep her self-respect.

Chapter Six

Now, that was what he was talking about. Blood watched Alizay retreat out the door and could have cackled with glee. Yes, she was distressed but he knew he could help her work through that shit. The point was, he'd finally cracked her icy exterior. Sure, she could come across sweet and innocent, but he'd had the feeling there was fire buried deep, and he'd been right. Now that he'd broken through that barrier, he could work on tearing it down completely. He wanted the little vixen for his own. He'd give her a little bit, then invade her private sanctuary. Then he'd seduce her into picking up where they left off.

"What the fuck did you do, Blood?" Alex entered the gym with Thorn. Neither man looked happy. "I stayed outside, trying to give you guys a little privacy, then Alizay ran out of here like her hair was on fire. What the fuck?"

"Relax," Blood said, grinning. "She just needs a bit to adjust."

"Adjust? To what?" Alex's tone of voice put Blood on alert.

He shrugged. "She wants me. She's just gotta figure out it's useless to fight me."

The second the words were out of his mouth, Blood knew he'd fucked up. Alex was on him in an instant. Thorn moved to intercept, but didn't prevent the other man from grabbing Blood by the throat and shoving him against the wall. Blood knew he could fight his way free if needed. Thanks to Alizay's exercises and the extent to which Blood had pushed himself, he was in the best shape of his life. His legs were close to sound and his body stronger than it had ever been.

"What did you do to her, you son of a bitch?" Alex was furious.

"You ain't her daddy, Alex. She's a grown woman. I didn't do anything to her she didn't participate in willingly. Her brain just caught up to her body and she panicked."

"Blood is a lot of things, Alex," Thorn said, laying a hand on Alex's shoulder, "but he'd never hurt a woman. Especially not in that way."

"Bullshit!" Alex looked Blood directly in the eyes then. "He's a player! He'd take whatever he wanted whether she wanted it or not. And, no, I don't mean by force. He'd charm her, make her think he wanted more than a quick roll in the hay, then he'd blaze." Alex looked as angry as he sounded. "I'm telling you right now, Blood. Alizay isn't the kind of woman you toy with. I thought the two of you might have found a connection during your rehab. I get that and I'm fine with it. Like you said, she's an adult. But she's still one of my people. My family. I may not be her daddy, but she's still under my protection. You may be tougher than me, stronger than me, but I have bigger guns. I'm also just the kind of bastard who could -- and would -- poison you in your fucking sleep if I thought that was the only way to fucking kill you."

"For crying out loud," Blood said, prying Alex's fingers from around his throat. "You're acting like she's some fragile little thing who can't take care of herself. She's one of the most capable people I've ever seen. Not to mention she's mopped the floor with me in here more than a few times. She don't want my advances, she won't accept them."

"You're not listening!" Alex paced in a circle like a big jungle cat. He took his time, obviously formulating what he wanted to say. "Look." He finally stopped, scrubbing a hand over his face. "Alizay is a very intelligent woman. She's hard working and quick thinking on her feet. But she's had to fight every step of the way to be the confident woman you're seeing now." He took a breath, looking away as if debating what to say next. Blood had the feeling he was about to learn what made little Ali tick. "When we found Alizay, she was... how do I explain?" he muttered. "Owned... by the Shaws."

"Shaws," Blood mused, trying to place the name, but unable to.

"A gang in the underbelly of Rockwell. Arkham's woman, Rain, fought to free women and girls from them while she was here."

"Yeah." Blood nodded. "I wasn't here when Bones rescued the boy in your household from the gangs below the city, but Arkham has told us about it many times. Man's proud of his woman."

"Exactly. Alizay was one of the many girls they had captive. From the time she was aware of her own actions, she was taught that her only value was her body and what she could provide with it." Alex stopped, letting his words sink in before continuing. "My estate manager, Mrs. McDonald, a woman I've known since I was a boy, brought her within our protection and worked with other women in our household to help her overcome that mentality. It's not that they made her embarrassed to have sex or taught her to avoid a sex life. They tried to get her to understand she didn't have to in order to be accepted and loved."

"So she's not allowed to have casual sex?" Blood was starting to get angry. One kind of brainwashing was just as bad as another.

"Not at all! Just be aware that casual sex for her is as complicated as any relationship. In her mind, she's always trying to figure out why she's doing it. Is it for herself? Is it to try to please someone else? Is she using sex to try to gain something for herself or someone else? There is nothing casual about it. At least, not for her. We all try to stay out of her business and would never confront her about her choices. But you can't expect her to react like other women you've been with. If you're not serious about her, if you're just wanting her to put in a good word with the doc to clear you --"

"You can stop right the fuck there. I've far surpassed every single goal they set. For both legs. I don't need that from her, and while I ain't above using sex as a distraction from time to time, I ain't usin' it to get in or out of work. Besides, she wants it just as much as I do. She's just nervous. Which I can fix."

Alex just stared at him. Finally, he pointed a finger at him. "Fine. But if you hurt her, Blood, if you drag her back down that path of self-destruction, I will kill you."

"You can try." Blood snagged a towel and headed for the showers. He acknowledged he had some things to fix with Alizay, but he'd do it his own way. He'd also make sure she knew he had no intention of using her to get clear of his therapy. Beyond that, he wasn't sure what he had to offer her. He could definitely show her a good time. She seemed to have liked his attention a whole hell of a lot.

Pleasure. He could offer her pleasure. That would have to do.

* * *

"Alizay? You in there?"

If she called out that, no, she wasn't in here, Alizay wondered if Blood would just go away. Not likely. So she just stayed quiet, huddled in the bathtub as she tried desperately to wash off his scent.

Another knock. "Alizay?" Silence. "I'm not going away until I talk to you."

She put her hands over her ears. This was so embarrassing.

Another knock, louder this time, like he was pounding on the door with his fist. "Alizay! Ain't askin' again."

She couldn't stand it any longer. "Go away! I'm busy!"

"Not that busy. Open up!" More pounding. "Not leavin' 'til I talk to you!"

"Would you keep it down? You'll disturb the whole house!"

"House is too fuckin' big to disturb with just me yellin'. Now, open the fuck up or I'm breakin' down the fuckin' door. That'll definitely disturb the whole house."

One thing Alizay had learned about Blood during the three months she'd been with him was that he was perfectly capable of breaking down that door and not batting an eyelash. And he definitely wouldn't care if she was in the bathtub naked or sitting in a chair fully dressed.

With a frustrated growl, Alizay hurried out of the tub, sloshing water in her wake. She snagged a towel and wrapped it around her. Just as she neared the door, it opened and Blood stepped inside like he owned the fucking place.

"What the hell? I was coming!"

"Not yet," he muttered, eying her hungrily.

Self-consciously, Alizay gripped the towel tighter. "This is not appropriate," she managed to get out indignantly. "I need to get dressed."

Blood nodded, stalking toward her. She took a step backward but raised her chin. "Regardless of what you think of me, Blood, I'm not an easy mark. Now get out of my home."

Blood didn't make a move to leave, but he did stop his advancement toward her. "Never thought you were easy, Ali. You're the hardest woman I know. In more ways than one." Finally, he took a breath and met her gaze. "We need to talk."

"You know what, Blood? Fuck you! This is my home. My private space. If I'd wanted you in here, I'd have invited you!"

"Get dressed and we'll talk about it."

She gave a frustrated growl. "You can't dictate to me!"

"Can and will, sweetheart. You either get dressed or we're having this conversation with you in a wet towel. Can't promise where that'll lead, but I'm sure it won't go as planned."

"How has no one killed you yet?"

"Because I never let anyone close enough to want to try." He looked her square in the eyes when he answered her. There was still that heated lust in his gaze, but something else, too. Something primal. Possessive, even.

Alizay took a half step back before stopping herself. If she showed weakness he'd pounce. If she didn't back off... would he take it as a sign to act on that hungry look on his face? She knew he wanted her. Had seen the look on many a man's face in the past. But somehow, this was different.

"What do you want from me?" Her voice was a whisper, and she couldn't look him in the eyes. She couldn't seem to put any demand behind it. Blood was different from any man she'd ever known. Until today, other than a few flirtatious remarks Alizay knew were meant only to tease and make light of situations when he was hurting, he'd never made any kind of unwanted advance on her. She felt guilty for pushing too hard. Had she overreacted?

"Not sure. But I want to find out." Blood scrubbed a hand over his mouth as he looked at her wet body. She was covered only by a towel over her breasts that barely reached mid-thigh.

She swallowed. The man definitely wanted to fuck her. Hell, she wanted to fuck him. But what happened after that? She didn't want to risk coming off like the girl she'd been when she'd lived under the city, owned by the Shaws gang. She didn't want to be known as being "easy." Not because she was opposed to sex. Because she didn't want anyone to think she was trying to use her body to gain favors. It had taken her years to understand that people in the real world, as she'd come to think of it, didn't trade sex for favors. If they did, they kept it quiet. It was a mark of shame. Didn't mean Alizay saw it that way, only that she recognized others often did. She didn't want to be that girl.

"You're right," she finally said, knowing when to retreat. "I need to get dressed."

He grinned, motioning to the couch. "I'll just wait here for you."

* * *

Fuck. He had to be so fucking careful. But how did he convince Alizay she could have a good time with him without giving her false hope of a relationship? He didn't want one. She couldn't want one. Not with him, anyway. Hell, she hated him. But she was definitely attracted to him, and there was nothing wrong with a healthy sex life.

Alizay returned a couple minutes later dressed in jeans and a large T-shirt. Her hair was up in a knot on top of her head. She still wouldn't meet his gaze as she took a seat in a chair across from him on the couch.

"Tell me what you're afraid of," Blood asked. "Best way for me to alleviate your fears is to know what they are."

"I'm not afraid of you," she said, her gaze snapping to his.

"Not of me, but of what I want. Why does sex scare you?"

"It doesn't." But Alizay dropped her gaze to her hands. "I know someone told you my story, so don't pretend they didn't."

"Ain't pretendin'. But I want to hear it from your angle."

Alizay shook her head once, as if she would refuse to answer him, then she sighed. "My mother was a gang whore for the Shaws when she got pregnant with me. Understand, it wasn't by choice. I have no idea how she got there or what she did before that life, but she was forced into that role. I was, too."

Blood's gut clenched. "How old?"

She didn't answer him, only looked away before she continued as if he hadn't spoken. "I was taught by my mother that survival meant understanding my worth to the gang. If I could please everyone who used me, I could eventually pick the men I was with. By doing that, I could get special privileges and control the situation better. It was a lesson I learned well.

Though I didn't always succeed in pleasing the men I was given to, I managed more often than not and used those talents as much as I could to make my life easier." She gave him a fierce look. "I'm not talking about my past more than that. But suffice it to say, when I was brought here, I had to learn a whole new set of rules. The first time I suggested to Mr. Ivanovich I'd be 'forever grateful' if he'd just let me stay, I thought he was gonna blow a gasket." Her voice was so soft Blood had to really listen to hear her. The bright red color sweeping up her neck and face told her embarrassment at that memory.

"What'd he say to you?" Blood had to tamp down the rage simmering just below the surface at the thought someone had hurt her feelings. Why, he had no idea. She was perfectly capable of taking care of herself.

"Not to me. But he was pretty harsh with Mrs. McDonald."

"I can't imagine that woman can't handle herself. Hell, can't imagine anyone giving her shit either." It was true the woman was mostly soft spoken and motherly, but it was hard to think anyone in the household could reprimand her in any way.

"Well, he was. Mrs. McDonald actually cried. She cried and hugged me and apologized over and over. Then she and Gloria proceeded to explain to me I didn't have to trade myself for anything here. They helped me pick an interest and helped me get through school. All the while, they reeducated me not to automatically offer sex when I wanted or needed something." She stood and began to pace, her agitation obvious. "My whole life, if I needed to make a transaction, I paid for it with sex. Do you realize how humiliating it was to realize that's not how normal people do things? I had no money! What was I supposed to think I should do?"

"Go to Azriel or Alex. Or Giovanni."

"That's what Mrs. McDonald said." Alizay finally flopped back down on the chair across from the couch where she started. Head in her hands, she looked utterly defeated. "So, now, here I am doing it again. Only, this time, I have to wonder if I started it because I wanted to know what sex was like when I really wanted it, or if you did in order to get me to talk the doctor into releasing you. Do you realize how messed up it is to think like that?" When she looked up, her eyes were damp with tears. She was genuinely distressed.

"OK," Blood said, leaning forward to rest his forearms on his legs. "One thing at a time. First, I don't need your blessing for the doc to release me. I've already exceeded every goal I set for myself, and those goals were way higher than the ones you set as my therapist. I'm in the best shape of my life. My recently injured leg is stronger than it ever was, and my old injury is about ninety-five percent of what it was before the injury. Which is much better than when we started. Second, I don't pay women for sex. Not in any way, shape or form. If you have sex with me, it's because we both want it." He waited until she looked up to meet his gaze. "Third? You said you wanted to see what it felt like to have sex when you really wanted it?" When she nodded, he continued. "That, my dear, is a healthy sex drive. You're a beautiful, desirable woman. You should want to fuck a man who turns you on. And there is nothing wrong with that. At fuckin' all."

She seemed to relax then, but looked no less miserable. "Well, at least that's something. I thought I'd messed up again."

"If anyone messed up, Alizay, it was me. I talked with Alex. He says you're not the kind of woman to have casual hookups because there is nothing about sex that is casual for you. But I think he's wrong. I think maybe, sometimes, you need to just follow your instinct. If you want it, go for it. Not as a way to pay for something, or to advance, or to get something you want. Purely for the joy of it. Because, I gotta tell ya, if you put the effort into it then sex can be a whole lot of fun. You just have to lay the ground rules before you start."

"Ground rules?"

"Yeah. Like, no strings attached. We have sex for the fun and pleasure of it, but we're not committed to each other." The second he said it, Blood knew he was a fucking liar. He'd lose his shit if she had sex with someone else.

"Why are you frowning?"

Girl was astute. Probably because she'd been his constant companion for the better part of three months.

"Because maybe that's not a good idea." He cleared his throat and tried again. "What about if we agree to not be with anyone else while we're exploring sex with each other? That way we don't muddy the waters."

She shrugged. "You're assuming we're going through with this. I'm not so sure."

"Why? I know you want me. You wouldn't have lost control like that if you didn't."

"Not saying I don't want you. I'm just not sure it's a good idea. Technically, you're still my patient.

And if I go to the doc now…" She trailed off and gave a helpless shrug. "You see the dilemma."

"Not a problem, sweetheart. I can go to the doc myself. Only reason I ain't already is because you're the best damned trainer I've ever had. I was just going for the other five percent on my old injury, but, honestly, it was just an excuse to be near you."

That must have been absolutely the right thing to say because she got a soft look on her face, and her body relaxed. A small smile tugged at her lips, but she didn't let it go completely.

"So, what do we do now?"

Blood smiled and stood, reaching for her hand. She took it and he tugged her to feet. "Now we go back downstairs. There's several members of my club and their ol' ladies I want you to meet."

Chapter Seven

How had she missed all the people coming into the manor? Blood led Alizay to the great room where there were probably fifty people. All of them laughing and joking. The women in the group were giggling and going through Christmas decorations. Not having grown up celebrating Christmas, Alizay sometimes forgot about the holiday. She'd grown to look forward to it on occasion, but this year, with everything going on with Blood, she'd completely forgotten about it.

"What day is it?" She had an overwhelming urge to find a calendar to see how much time she had to prepare. She might not have grown up with Christmas, but she understood its importance to the people around her. Always, she tried to make sure she gave Mrs. McDonald and Grace something special. She'd have never made it as far as she had if not for them. She tried to give something to the men of the house, but what did you get people who had everything? So, each year, she'd settled on making something for each of them. It wasn't much, but it was all she had.

"November twenty-seventh," Blood said.

"OK. So I've got time. When's Thanksgiving?"

He gave her an odd look, then smothered a grin. "Yesterday, sweetheart."

"Yesterday?" The bottom fell out of her world, and she covered her cheeks with her hands. "Ohmigod! I missed it! Mrs. McDonald will be so disappointed."

"Settle down, sweetheart. It's not the end of the world." Blood gently pulled her hands from her face. Alizay was close to tears.

"She says it's important for family to sit down to Thanksgiving together. Even the bosses join us."

"You were helping your patient. Surely Mrs. McDonald will understand."

With a heavy sigh, Alizay put her shoulders back. "I'll have to apologize to her. In the meantime, I'm assuming you brought me here for a reason?"

"I did. Come with me." He extended a hand and Alizay took it, letting him guide her where he wanted.

They approached the smiling, laughing women. It looked like there had been an explosion of tinsel. One young woman, sitting in the middle, seemed to be the cause of the explosion as she excitedly giggled as she pulled out one decoration after another, most involving garland and lights. Loads of lights. The only male in the whole group was a brooding man with a short beard and shaggy hair that looked like he'd gone without a haircut for six months or more.

The small woman with all the garlands suddenly jumped to her feet and wrapped a red-and-silver one around the big guy's neck, threw her arms around him, and kissed him soundly. Everyone laughed. The big guy just slid his arms around the woman and let her arrange the garland as she wished, never saying a word. When she turned her back to dig more in the box of decorations, he gave her a soft, affectionate smile. Clearly, the man adored his woman.

"Suzie," Blood called. The woman she'd been watching looked up, her smile still radiant. "Will you take care of my woman?" He urged Alizay forward. "This is Alizay. She needs someone to show her the finer points of decorating for Christmas. Do not spare the glitter."

Alizay started, looking at him sharply. *His woman*? "Blood." She tugged at his arm, trying to pull him away from the group. "What are you doing?"

"Hello, Alizay." Suzie was up on her feet in an instant, rushing toward her. Before Alizay could protest, Suzie wrapped her arms around her and gave her a fierce hug. "Welcome to the family! This is Angel, my mom, and Fleur, Beast's wife. Over there is Zora and Darcy, Data's woman and daughter respectively. Darcy is also Viper's ol' lady. That's Magenta. She belongs to Sword, and Rain over there is Arkham's woman." She took a breath before continuing. "Luna is with Bohannon, Spring is with Havoc, Helen is with Trucker, Ambrosia is Torpedo's, Lucy belongs to Vicious, Mariana is with Thorn, and Stunner --" she turned to the big shaggy headed man with all the glittery tinsel --"is mine."

"Notice how she said we all belong to the men, but Stunner belongs to her," Angel said, offering her hand to Alizay. "This is a big bunch, but we're family. Don't try to keep everyone straight all at once. Suzie gets a bit excited this time of year and steamrolls through everything." She pulled the younger woman into a hug, squeezing her and smiling affectionately.

"And we love her for it," Cain said as he approached, reaching for his daughter and giving her a solid bear hug. He nodded to Blood. "Glad you're joining us."

Blood stiffened, but nodded at the other man. "Still pissed at you."

Cain shrugged. "Figured you would be. Good thing I made up for you nearly gettin' killed by securing you the best nurse and physical therapist we could find." He grinned at Alizay. "Looks like the two of you are gettin' along." Cain extended his hand for her to shake. Alizay smelled a trap, but took his hand obediently. "You know I've got you hired for the next month, right? Azriel is lettin' us all crash here until

Christmas. Both clubs." He grinned. "Blood don't treat you right, you come to me or Angel. I'll lay him out for ya."

Some of that even made sense. Alizay had no idea whether to be uncomfortable or relieved. When Suzie threw herself into Alizay's arms, squealing, however, Alizay just tried to focus on staying on her feet.

"You're going to love everybody!" Suzie said. "They've already put the little kids to bed, but you'll meet them tomorrow. They're all so wonderful. They'll love you, and you'll love them."

"I've never been around kids," Alizay said, automatically looking to Blood for support. "I-I won't know what to say."

Suzie hesitated just that little bit. Instantly, Stunner was at her side. "Nothin' to worry about. They generally take care of the sayin'. Hard to get a word in, usually."

Blood put a steadying hand on Alizay's shoulder. "You'll be fine. Just get to know everyone tonight. I'll come get you when it's time to go to bed."

Alizay wasn't exactly sure how to go about getting to know the rowdy bunch. Sure, she lived in the mansion with the rest of the household under the protection of the Shadow Demons, but she spent most of her time at the hospital or in the field. Her interaction skills were lacking in most areas. And that was only the women she worried about. The men gathered by themselves -- except Stunner -- and let the women have free rein over the Christmas decoration plans. Apparently, they were just going through boxes and deciding what they wanted to use. No one was doing anything until the children were there to help. The fact this was a pre-decorating event didn't seem to deter from the excitement and happiness and just pure joy of the occasion. At least, that was the way it seemed to Alizay. It was at once exhilarating and overwhelming.

She did her best to keep up with all the conversations going on around her. Most of it was questions for her until she felt like she was being interrogated. Suzie found her gaze and smiled softly at her. She looked up at Stunner and said something, then made her way to Alizay.

"We're sometimes a little much to take, though this is the more reserved bunch. The guys tend to get really boisterous. Are you OK?"

"I try to stay away from crowds of men. Maybe I'm just not used to crowds of any kind." Alizay smiled to try to soften her words. "I'm sorry."

"Oh, no! Don't be!" Suzie put her arm through Alizay's and guided her to the bar. Suzie went around behind it and pulled out a can of vanilla cream soda and a bottle of butterscotch schnapps. "Maybe it will help loosen you up a bit." She winked at Alizay as she poured a generous amount of the sweet liquor over ice followed by the cream soda before pushing the glass toward Alizay. "Taste it."

Alizay could see why the woman was so well loved by everyone. Her smile could light up the world, and she was so sensitive to the people around her. She took a sip of the concoction before her eyes widened and she took another, bigger drink. "Oh, my!"

"I know, right?"

They both giggled. Suzie made herself one and refilled Alizay's before they left the bar. "I find a little alcohol goes a long way with get-togethers with strangers." Suzie smiled. "After a couple of these, you won't care so much about everyone else."

"I can't argue with that."

Suzie looked at her a long moment. Alizay started to get uncomfortable before the other woman spoke. "You're not Blood's woman yet. Are you?"

Alizay shrugged, her stomach immediately tightening. "No." Her response was quiet. In the gym, she was confident. In the field and the hospital, she could even be forceful and commanding. In a social situation? She didn't stand a chance.

"You know, he really likes you. Stunner said Cain noticed the changes soon after you started working with him."

Alizay smiled. "Maybe. Doesn't mean I like him back."

Suzie giggled. "You totally like him. When you walked in here, you looked at him for reassurance with the crowd. You still look for him, even though you've been with us a good hour and know we won't bite. He keeps an eye on you, too, you know."

Naturally, Alizay had to look up to find Blood. Sure enough, he was looking straight at her. "Shit," she said, gulping her drink. Suzie just giggled again.

"I'll get you another one."

An hour later, with Alizay and Suzie back in the Christmas decorations with the other women, Alizay was pleasantly buzzed and growing increasingly aroused. Blood kept looking at her. She kept looking at him. Which prompted her to have another drink. Butterscotch schnapps? Goooood... Alizay drained her glass with a gasp, setting it on a nearby table. The second she did, Blood tipped back the last of his beer and stalked toward her.

"Uh oh," Suzie whispered to her. "Looks like you're leaving now."

She so was. Just the intent way Blood looked at her said he was getting her out of here. It struck her then that she was more than ready. For the first time in her life, she was going to have sex with the man of her choosing. And it was going to be Blood.

He stood over her, looming. Strangely, she didn't feel threatened or intimidated in any way. All she felt was anticipation. He held out his hand and she took it. Helping her to her feet seemed to be an effortless task. Then he tugged her after him and they left the room.

The walk to her room was a blur. It seemed like the closer they got, the faster they went. All she could think about was what was about to happen. She was really going to do this. Would he think less of her? Would the other members of his club? What about Mrs. McDonald or the bosses?

No! She wasn't going there. Mrs. McDonald and Gloria had both told her if she wanted to have sex, it should be because it was what she wanted. Not what she thought someone wanted of her or because she wanted something in exchange. This was about nothing more than the experience -- and wanting it with Blood and no one else.

The second the door was shut, Blood pulled her into her arms. He didn't kiss or pull at her clothes, but held her tightly. His body seemed to shudder around her, his cock throbbing insistently against her belly. "Fuck," he whispered, dropping a kiss into her hair. "Ain't nothin' 'bout you that don't appeal to me."

"I feel the same way." Alizay knew her words were spoken softly. Hell, he probably couldn't hear her.

Blood pulled back, gripping her by the shoulders and leaning down to look her directly in the eyes. "Tell me you really want this," he demanded. "That you want me."

"I do, Blood. More than I've ever wanted anything in my life."

"We do this, I'm telling you right now I want more than a night. I want time to see if we can have something more permanent. That means I don't have other women. You don't have other men. I only say that because I'm not a hypocrite, and I know I'll never be able to have anything casual with you. I thought I could, but it ain't happenin'."

"Why did you tell your club I was your woman?" She had to know. Of all the things she imagined him saying, his response surprised her.

"Because I wanted every single man anywhere around to know you were taken. I find I'm a possessive bastard when it comes to you, and I didn't want there to be any misunderstandings."

Alizay surprised herself by letting out a bark of laughter. Blood just grinned at her, then bent to kiss her. His touch was filled with passion and fire. Need. Alizay felt the answering need in herself, something boiling up inside her she had no hope of containing. She'd been doubting herself, wondering if this was what she really wanted. Was there was something she secretly wanted from Blood she was willing to trade her body for? Something she hadn't yet admitted to herself? What she realized was, giving her body to him wasn't just the means to the end. This *was* the end game. She'd wanted to experience sex with a man of her choosing? Well, her choice was Blood.

It didn't take long for him to get her shirt off. Alizay worked on her pants quickly while he shed his own clothing. She started to pull her sports bra over her head when Blood stopped her.

He stood before her in his boxer briefs, all that defined, heavy muscle on full display. She'd seen hard men before. Men who were strong and rough and blatantly sexy, but no one she'd ever seen had the blatant sex appeal Blood had. She wanted to lick every ridge and hollow, every single inch of all that delicious skin then nip him with her teeth just to leave her mark on him for every woman in his club to know he was taken.

"You don't want an exclusive relationship, Alizay, you need to say so now. I'm dead serious about what I said. Once I have you, I'm gonna want more. I don't share."

"Well, I don't share either," she countered. "So, exclusive better mean exclusive."

He grinned. "I guess you'll just have to make sure all the club girls know you've claimed me."

Challenge fucking accepted.

* * *

This hadn't been part of his grand plan, but Blood was on the verge of losing himself. And he hadn't even started playing with her yet.

Alizay wrapped her lithe arms around his neck and kissed him as hungrily as he kissed her. Somehow he managed to get them to the bed, though that was about as much as he could do. He stopped her from removing her bra because he knew once she exposed what he knew would be lovely breasts, he would spend the rest of the night worshiping them. While that idea had merit, this first time he wanted her to lose herself in him. He wanted to give her the most spectacular orgasm she'd ever had.

As he saw it, pleasure was the key to winning her. If she wanted to give her body to him, she'd be all in. Somehow, some way, Blood knew he was keeping her. Forever. She was a remarkable woman, strong of body and mind. He might not be her equal, but he was damned well not letting her find someone who was. He was just that big a bastard. She was his. "Tellin' you straight, sweetheart. Ain't fuckin' you yet."

A look of hurt and confusion crossed her face, and she opened her mouth to say something, probably to protest. Or to tell him to go to hell. He cut her off. "What I am gonna do is worship this little body of yours until you scream. Then worship it some more. After that, if you come hard for me, I'll think about fuckin' you."

"Oh..." The shocked look on her face was priceless. Blood took that opportunity to strip her bra over her head. As expected, her breasts were exquisite. Small, but perky with a fine layer of muscle underneath. Also, as predicted, he couldn't waste the opportunity to taste. The second his lips closed over one puckered nipple, Alizay gave a little cry and her fingers immediately threaded through his hair.

As he sucked, she cried out, alternately pulling his hair then clutching his head to her as if she couldn't make up her mind if she liked what he was doing. Blood knew she loved it by the way her legs tightened around him. He could practically feel the moist heat of her pussy through her panties where her pussy rubbed against his belly. He could have happily stayed there in bed with his mouth fused to her lush tit all fucking day, because she was sweet as fucking sugar.

Blood resisted tightening his arms around her. The need for more was there but he intended to keep going like this, not stopping until his mouth was fused to her glistening cunt.

Her breath left her chest in a little rush when he pulled away, taking her nipple with the suction of his mouth until it slipped free with a little pop. Blood held her gaze as he inched down her body, leaving kisses and little nips in his wake. Her belly was so flat he had to make an effort to nip her stomach below her navel. Just to tease her more, he swirled his tongue in her belly button.

"Love to see this sexy little thing pierced," he rasped. "Those pouty nipples as well."

"Ain't happening, big guy," she breathed, but there was color to her cheeks. Blood thought she might be more inclined to it than she wanted to admit.

"Then, what about..." He pulled her panties to the side, tracing his finger up and down the seam of her pussy until he found her clit. "...this little bit? Oh, the things I could do to you if you had a ring in your clit."

"Ah! Blood!" Her pussy twitched as he put his face right next to it. He was sure she could feel his breath over the sensitive bud as he spoke.

"You like the sound of that?"

"I -- I don't know." Her eyes were wide, her face flushed. Blood knew he was pushing her, but he needed to know what she liked and what put her off. If he had a normal conversation with her, she might balk if she wanted kinky things, thinking it was what he wanted to hear.

"Hum," he said as he took another long, slow lick of her clit. It pulsed under his tongue. "This little clit says you might." Again, he stroked the seam of her pussy with a finger and held it up to her. "This wet little cunt says the same thing."

"That's not fair," she wailed. "You're not giving me a chance to think about it!"

"And if you could, would you tell me the truth? I'm a kinky bastard, Alizay. I love sex in all its forms. If you truly don't like something, we'll talk about it. See what the problem is. If it just doesn't do it for you that's one thing, but if you don't like it simply because you're afraid I'll think less of you, then we've got a problem."

"Blood, stop," she said, trying to push him away. "I need to think."

"No, baby. You need to feel."

"No!"

He stopped what he was doing but didn't move or let her up. "Alizay, look at me." When she met his gaze, he continued. "Ain't gonna lie. I've always been into extreme sex. I'll want to fuck you every chance you let me. I'll want to tie you up. Want to discipline you." Again, she shivered under him. "I'll want to fuck your ass, plug it while I fuck your pussy. I may even put a collar on you and lead you around like my pet. Or, better yet, spread your pussy with a ring. Leash that little ring. Lead you by your pussy."

She let out a loud groan before putting her forearm over her eyes.

"Oh no, baby." Blood denied her being able to hide from him. He snagged her wrist and brought both her hands down to restrain them. "You don't get to hide from me. I want to do all that. But only if it turns you on. If it doesn't, I'll keep suggesting things until I find something that does."

"I don't understand. All that is depraved! No woman likes doing that stuff!"

He grinned. "There's where you're wrong, sweetheart. Some women can't let themselves go enough to like it. Whether by conditioning in their upbringing, or just because their personality is a little reserved, they just aren't open to it. Some women secretly want to try it but either can't open up enough to ask for it, or have partners who are opposed. Others love it. A lot. What you have to keep in mind is, it's all for mutual fun. If you don't like it, I ain't doin' it."

"So, it's not wrong?" She looked at him like he was the person she was going to with all her questions about sex and would believe what he told her. Maybe it was because she had trusted him this far. Maybe because she wanted him, or just a normal relationship with a man in general. Whatever her reasons were, Blood was glad he was the one she trusted.

"Not at all, baby. I'm not going to lie to you. What we do in private is our own business, but yeah. Some people would put you down for it. I ain't one of those people. You'll have to make up your own mind about everyone else in the club or this house. The club girls at Bane are down for pretty much anything, but most of them do it for power. They want a patched member in their bed, thinking they'll have status or ranking among the other women. They might give you shit if they found out what we do together, but ain't none of them ever balked at anything a man in the club wanted."

He held her gaze and kissed her clit once.

"My advice to you about that is to keep it to yourself unless you trust the person you're telling. That's pretty much the way the ol' ladies do it." He grinned. "Though, ain't a single one of them except maybe Suzie who'd give a shit. She wouldn't care, she'd just blush and cover her ears. Unfortunately, when she does that, Stunner has a shit-eatin' grin on his face so we all know she's just embarrassed. Hell, Vicious's ol' lady sometimes fucks him at club parties. And she's the one who starts it."

"Mrs. McDonald said if it was something I wanted it was OK. I just wasn't supposed to do have sex with anyone to gain something material. To trade sex for something."

"I suppose that's right. Though, it's all a matter of perspective. She didn't want you to feel like you had to use sex to keep a home here. Right?"

"Something like that," she said, her gaze darting away.

"You ain't' gotta worry about that now. Not only do you have a valuable skill, but you've got a man who ain't lettin' you go." He licked at her pussy again, giving her a wink. "And you can do anything you want with him. In fact, he insists on it."

"Sex. Any time I want it."

"Exactly."

She let out a happy little giggle. "Thank God. I was beginning to think I'd never be able to have sex again."

"So, you like sex, huh?"

"Sometimes. There were a couple of men I didn't mind. Mostly because even when they were making me do what they wanted, they always made sure I got something out of it, too."

"Much as I'm grateful you didn't have all bad experiences, ain't gonna talk about you with other men. Too much of a jealous bastard for that."

"Then, for my first demand of you…" She grinned. "…why don't you just shut the hell up and fuck me already?"

Blood chuckled as he covered her pussy with his mouth once more. His tongue stabbed deep, penetrating her and licking inside her as far as he could reach. He shook his head a little, his nose rubbing her clit while his tongue fucked her. Beautiful little cries came from Alizay as she thrashed beneath his touch. Yeah. He'd been right. There was a little hellcat inside her waiting to be unleashed, and Blood intended to do it. Starting right now.

Chapter Eight

Sex had always been a means to an end. Alizay hadn't been lying when she told Blood she'd sometimes enjoyed it. She had. It seemed like forever since she'd gotten off by anything other than her own hand, and she'd forgotten how good it could be.

In a way, she'd fought the pleasure she sometimes felt. To her, it had signaled she was giving in to what the Shaws wanted of her. To be a whore for them. But, once free of them, she'd found a burning need inside her for the pleasure she sometimes found in the act she'd grown to hate. Sometimes, at night when she was alone, she'd use her phone to look up porn of all kinds. Some of it had repulsed her, but some...hadn't. She'd masturbated to those scenes over and over, trying to mute her desires so she didn't do anything to embarrass Mrs. McDonald or her friend, Grace.

Looking at it from the perspective Blood had outlined here -- and the one Mrs. McDonald had explained -- perhaps she'd gone too far the other way. All she knew was, when Blood thrust two fingers inside her pussy, it didn't feel wrong. It felt all too right.

"That's it, precious," Blood crooned to her as he finger-fucked her. "I can tell you like it because you're so fuckin' wet."

"Yes," she breathed. "So good..."

Alizay decided in that moment, she was going to just go with it. She trusted Blood with this, with her body. She'd let him lead the way. If he wanted her to try something, she'd do it. And there wasn't a doubt in her mind he could make it good for her. He knew his club. He knew her fears. She'd been with him for a solid three months and, in that time, she'd learned several things about him. Nothing in his character suggested he'd be the type of man to humiliate her. Quite the opposite. He was protective, almost to a fault. Having resolved herself to this, Alizay opened herself wide to him, letting him have anything he wanted. It felt right.

"Oh, yeah, baby. That's it." Blood's voice was like a third hand to caress her with. Just that husky, sexy note had her pussy creaming again. "You're givin' yourself to me, aren't you?"

"Yes. I trust you."

"Good. Now, come for me."

"I -- what?"

"Come for me, Alizay."

"But... I'm not... OH!"

Blood fluttered her clit with his tongue while thrusting his fingers deep. Everything crashed over Alizay like a tidal wave. All his sexy talk, all her pent-up need -- everything conspired to take her sanity in one powerful, wet rush. She screamed her pleasure, hooking her hands behind her knees and pulling them higher, giving him as much access to her as he wanted. Between her legs, Blood growled and slurped, seeming to love her orgasm as much as she did.

When she finally came down from the pleasure high, Blood had shucked his underwear and was retrieving a condom from his jeans pocket. A smile tugged at Alizay's lips, and she let it. So far, this was turning into the experience of a lifetime.

"Fuck, you're sexy," he growled as he sheathed his cock. "Pussy wet and dripping. Lips all swollen from me eatin' you. Little clit still pulsing. Fuckin' needy little thing, aren't you?"

He knelt between her legs, fisting his cock as he grazed it up and down her pussy lips. "You want my cock?"

"Yes," she breathed, her body tense. "Put it in me. Fuck me with it."

His eyes sparkled at her. "That's it," he said with a grin. "That's what I want to hear from you."

He tucked the head into her opening. Alizay met his gaze boldly, lifting her chin even as her breath came in little pants. "Do it!" She hissed.

Blood gave her a lopsided grin before easing himself down on top of her and thrusting slowly inside her tight body. The burn was exquisite. Alizay thrust her pelvis at him, trying to get him in deeper, but Blood just grinned at her.

"Uh uh, baby. We're doin' this my way, and I say we're goin' slow. You're so tight, I want to ease you into it."

"I'm burning," she gasped. "So good! Blood, it burns, but it's… it's wonderful!"

"Good," he purred in her ear, nudging her hair aside to lick at the shell before nipping the lobe. "I want you to come so hard. Come on my cock until you take me with you."

Alizay felt her pussy squeeze around his dick like she wanted to strangle him. Truth was, she had very little control over her body now. Any other time she'd been so helpless, panic had overwhelmed her, but this was different. She knew she could get away from Blood if she wanted. It was her body that was out of control. The pleasure wasn't something she was accustomed to. Not like this. Even with her own hand she'd never felt anything as wonderful as what Blood gave her.

She wrapped her legs around his waist again, digging her heels into his ass. Her fingers threaded through his hair and she pulled him down to her, needing to kiss him while he took her body. The little whimper that escaped her was swallowed by his satisfied groan as he began to move faster at her urging. Alizay was rapidly approaching the point where she could no longer control herself. She found herself clawing at his back as she kissed him. When she nipped his lower lip sharply, he growled at her.

"Little witch! Trying to make me come before I'm ready? That your plan?"

"I just want you to fuck me," she whimpered. "Need it so much!"

Blood raised himself on one arm, griping one breast with his free hand and twisting the nipple sharply. She cried out, arching her back, needing more of that. The pain was the perfect contrast to the pleasure, threatening to tip her over the edge into oblivion.

She dug her nails into his arms and her heels into his ass, using all the leverage she could to fuck him, to make him go faster. A scream of frustration escaped her, then she bit down on his shoulder. Hard.

"Fuck! Fuck!" Blood pounded into her, his speed and intensity increasing to a ferocious crescendo. "Come, Alizay! Do it now!"

"Blood!" Alizay was helpless to do anything other than what Blood commanded. She came, her muscles tightening around his dick until her cunt ached and throbbed. Her scream was loud and long, the orgasm continuing on and on until her body finally went limp. How had he done this to her? How had he so completely taken over her body and tuned it to his? Did she even care?

Blood rolled them over so they lay on their sides, him still inside her. His cock gave the occasional pulse, as did her pussy. Alizay was limp as a dishrag. Had this happened at any other time in her life, she'd panic because death would have surely followed. Not this time. Blood's arms were tight around her, his body surrounding her protectively.

"You good?"

"Mm hm," she murmured.

"Give me a minute," he panted, "and I'll get us cleaned up."

"Ummm," she purred. Yeah. This was heaven.

"My little Alizay's pleased?"

"Ummm hummm."

Blood chuckled. "You rest. I'll take care of everything and we'll rest. Tomorrow will be long and tiring, but I promise you'll enjoy every second of it."

Alizay froze. "You mean, with the others. Downstairs?"

"Yup."

"I really have to go to that?"

Blood chuckled. "You really do. Suzie would be devastated if you didn't."

She really liked Suzie. "I wouldn't hurt her feelings for anything, but I just want to stay with you."

"Don't worry. I'll be there. You need me, all you have to do is look up and I'll come for you."

Alizay sighed. "I suppose I can manage."

"Of course you can. Stay here. I'll be right back."

Blood was only gone a couple of minutes. When he returned, he had a warm, wet cloth he used to wash her ever so gently. Then he tossed the cloth in the general direction of the bathroom and climbed into bed with her.

"Sleep," he said, sounding like he was half there already.

"I think I can manage that. Not sure I can ever remember being so… exhausted."

Blood's warm chuckle filled her with contentment. "That's exactly what I want to hear. Rest, sweetheart. I've got you."

Alizay closed her eyes and promptly fell asleep.

* * *

The next day was filled with so much merriment and activity Alizay looked positively terrified. At first. Then she seemed to throw herself into all the decorating and dancing and baking. Blood was proud of the way she adapted when he knew how uncomfortable she had to be. Still, she managed to laugh and sing with the rest of the women. Suzie in particular took a shine to her. The women were about the same age and both probably felt a connection to each other, sensing something deep inside them was alike.

Both Salvation's Bane and Bones members mingled with the household of the Shadow Demons. The Demons, though they often hired the men of ExFil, who were all part of one or the other MC, weren't MC themselves. They sometimes tried to pattern their behavior after the more rough and tumble clubs, but Shadow Demons were mercenaries more than anything else. Not only that, but the leaders of the Demons were three of the richest men in the country. While Cain had an abundance of wealth, as did more than one of the Salvation's Bane members, Alexi, Azriel, and Giovanni were in a league outside of all of them put together. They owned the biggest tech company in the world, having contracts with the richest nations.

Even though the Demons' household was used to less boisterous gatherings, everyone seemed to be having a wonderful time. Alizay included. Blood was near her most of the time, but let her have space when she ventured away from him. Right now, she and Suzie were busy stringing lights and garlands over the fireplace mantel. Several children, including those belonging to couples at Bane and Bones, were giggling as they made stockings for hanging after Suzie and Alizay were finished.

"I hope we get to decorate Daddy's clubhouse like we did this one." Blood had to cover his mouth with his hand to prevent anyone from seeing his amusement. Willa, the daughter of Trucker and Helen at Bones, was just too cute for words. If Cain wanted to let the little imps decorate the Bones clubhouse -- which he would -- that was up to him. Blood was just glad Thorn had no such problems setting his foot down with his own daughter. Little Sonya was only four but a holy terror when she wanted to be. Which was often.

"Daddy said I could have the biggest tree in the whole universe!" Speak of the devil. "It'll be much bigger than this one," Sonya boasted. The girl might be only four, but she was already as competitive as they came. "Our clubhouse will have way more lights than this."

Willa narrowed her eyes. "We'll have lights all over the inside and outside at Bones."

Sonya, not to be out done by the older girl, came back with, "Our outside trees will have lights."

"I'm puttin' lights on all the bikes. Daddy said I could."

OK, that wasn't so cute. "Who said you'd be puttin' lights on the bikes?" Trucker had been half listening to the kids as he sipped a beer. His ol' lady, Helen, was helping the smaller children string together popcorn and dried fruit to make a colorful garland for the tree. She glanced up briefly at her husband, her lips twitching. Trucker was now at complete attention.

The girl didn't bat an eyelash or hesitate in her answer. "Why, Mommy, of course."

"That wasn't what you just said, Willa. You said I gave you permission."

"Maybe you heard wrong." She cocked her head to the side, looking far older than her seven years. "You are getting old, you know."

"What the fu-, er, fudge, Helen?" Apparently, the big bad biker wasn't keen on swearing in front of his daughter. Or it could have been his ol' lady's raised eyebrow.

"Don't look at me," Helen said. "I'd never encourage any of the children to touch any of your brothers' precious bikes. I know how deeply you feel about them." Rumor had it Trucker and Helen had been arguing about this very topic. Apparently, Helen had asked Trucker to teach her to ride, and he'd politely declined. Might have been phrased something like "Are you outta your fuckin' mind?" But it was more polite than Blood would have been. At least, that's what he told himself. Looking at Alizay, watching her observe the byplay intently, he knew he'd give the woman any fucking thing she wanted as long as it made her happy. Including teaching her to ride his bike.

Trucker looked at his daughter sternly. "Are you fibbing to me, little Miss Willa?"

The seven-year-old actually shrugged. "Well, she didn't actually give us permission, but she said she'd love to see the look on your face if we did. So I'm gonna do it. Cause I love to see my mommy happy." She grinned up at Trucker. Little brat looked smug about it, too. Definitely going to cause trouble, that one.

"That's it. We're going home." Trucker looked as disgruntled as a biker could.

"Uh huh," Helen said. "Go ahead and pack, big guy."

Trucker turned back to the bar. "What're you lookin' at?"

The thin man, dressed in the Demons' staff uniform, just shrugged and popped the top on another beer, giving Trucker a grin as he set it in front of him. "Not sure. But my guess is a whipped biker."

Everyone within earshot roared with laughter.

Blood grinned. Alizay laughed along with everyone else, looking more and more relaxed. She was still a bit reserved, but Suzie's laugh and enthusiasm were infectious. Alizay didn't stand a chance.

As if she heard his thoughts, Alizay looked up, her gaze finding his unerringly. Her face, which had been bright with a delighted smile, relaxed. The soft look on her face as she mouthed "Thank you" to him made his chest ache. The heat in her eyes as her gaze lingered did the same to his cock.

Feeling a little wicked, Blood crooked his finger at her, beckoning Alizay to him. She stood and crossed the distance to him slowly, her hips swaying seriously with every step.

"You look good enough to eat," he growled. She blushed becomingly.

"It's funny," she mused. "Just a moment ago, I was sitting back, enjoying being with everyone. Then you looked at me."

He raised an eyebrow. "That made you not enjoy this?"

"Not at all! It…" She leaned into him, clutching his shirt in her hands, her body trembling against his. "It made me want you."

Blood's arms, which had loosely embraced her when she'd come to him, tightened around her, needing her close enough to feel his steely erection. "I know the feeling." He nipped her ear gently as he spoke. "I could lift you to the bar, strip your pants off, and eat you right here."

"Blood!" Her body still trembled, but she stiffened against him as well.

He froze. "What is it, baby?"

"I…" She buried her face against his chest. "Please… please don't do that here. The children…"

"Baby, look at me." He made his tone firm, knowing she would resist. He'd embarrassed her unintentionally. Sure, he loved to push her. He'd pushed her often enough with this, and she seemed to like it, but he never wanted her to feel uncomfortable around him. Especially not about sex. As expected, she just shook her head, and her body trembled with her silent sobs. "Ali." He put a warning in his voice this time. "Look at me, now." When she reluctantly did, he framed her face with his big hands. "I would never take you in front of children. Ever. Also, as much as I like teasin' you with it in private, I'd never take you in public. Not because I don't want everyone in the Goddamn world to know who's fuckin' you, but because you can't do it. That's a hard limit for you and I know it."

"But I never said --"

"Honey, you didn't have to. You told me your past. Fuckin' you in front of everyone is something men did from your old life. This is your new one. A new relationship meant to build you up. Not tear you down. While you'll find that the men and women in Bane don't care who sees them fuckin', you care. That's all that matters to me."

"Have you done that with other women?" Her voice was soft, and she could hardly look at him, but she managed to hold his gaze. Blood was prouder of her than he could say.

"I have. Enjoyed it. But with you, not only do I have a need to protect you, I'm jealous as fuck. Don't want no one seeing this perfect, perfect body but me. Also, don't want no misunderstandings. You're mine. Once you're comfortable enough to wear my property patch, I won't worry so much, but right now, I ain't havin' some dumbass prospect hittin' on my woman just because he's drunk and I've shown you off at a fuckin' party."

"So, all that talk of piercing my clit and leading me around by it? That was just dirty talk?" Did she look... disappointed?

He gave her a wicked grin, his cock near bursting at that fucking image. "Didn't say that. Only that I wouldn't do it in public."

"Oh God." Alizay sagged against him, whimpering softly. "Blood, I need..."

"I know, baby. Let's get the fuck outta here."

They made it down the hall and around the corner. Blood glanced inside the gym quickly and, seeing no one, he pulled Alizay inside with him. He shut and locked the door then jogged to the shower room to make sure they were truly alone.

"Come here." He reached for her, not giving her time to comply with his order. He didn't have the patience. "Need you." She gasped as he fastened his mouth to hers, taking her with a brutal kiss.

* * *

Alizay couldn't remember ever having been so turned on. Knowing what he could do with her body, she was even hornier than she'd been the first time they'd had sex. His touch was rough as he jerked her shirt up and dug under her bra to grip her breast, squeezing roughly. It was just shy of too much, but the slight discomfort only added to her need.

She found the waistband of his jeans and shoved her hand inside, gripping his cock and squeezing, milking him.

"Fuck!" Blood ducked away from her, spinning her around and slamming her against the wall. His body was hot and hard, aggressively pinning her. One big hand held hers against the wall above her head while the other fumbled with her pants, shoving them over her hips.

With a grunt, Blood pulled her hips back but kept her hands mashed against the wall so that she was bent slightly at the waist. There was a pause where Alizay could hear him fumbling with his own pants, then he rammed inside her with a brutal thrust.

She cried out, but arched her back and bucked into him. Blood fucked her hard. Mercilessly. And Alizay reveled in it.

"Fuck me!" she cried. "Do it hard!"

Blood smacked her ass. "I'll fuck you how I wanna fuck you, woman." He let go of her hands to bunch his fist in her hair. Alizay gasped, the pain tempering her pleasure the perfect amount to keep her on the edge without letting her fall. All the while, Blood pounded inside her. Each thrust seemed to get harder, making for a teeth-clattering ride.

Finally, he tugged her up by her hair, wrapping an arm around her waist and one over her chest. He shoved her against the wall with his body, continuing to fuck her.

"Fucking witch," he hissed at her ear. "Controlling me with my dick? I'll definitely pierce your little pussy. See how you like being controlled." Still he drove into her. His pace quickened as his arms tightened around her. "You'll be my pet. I'll sit you at my feet and make you beg for my cock." Alizay whimpered as he continued. "My own little kitten, hungry for my cream."

"Just know that, if I have to beg you for it, I have claws. I don't get what I want, I'll be using them."

"Goddamn…" he panted. "Mother fuck!" His cock pulsed inside her with every stroke. His hand slid down to her clit and he pinched it roughly between his fingers.

Alizay screamed. Loudly. Her orgasm crashed over her, making her buck even harder. She thrashed under him so he had to grip both her hips to continue to fuck her. Flesh slapped together loudly. Their gasps and moans grew louder and louder until Alizay came a second time, and Blood pushed himself hard and deep one last time. His cum exploded from him in a scalding rush, bathing her cunt inside. His weight alone held her up, mashing her between himself and the wall. Sweat clung to Alizay's body and she fought for breath.

Finally, with a tenderness that belied the sex they'd just had, Blood tugged up her pants and turned her around, enfolding her tightly in his strong arms.

"Fuck," he whispered. "Just… fuck!"

Alizay giggled. "Agreed."

He lifted his head, urging her to look at him. "I didn't hurt you, did I?"

"No, Blood." She smiled up at him. "That was the most fun I've ever had."

"You know I'd never really hurt you though. Right? I like to talk during sex. Like to think about stuff like that, but I'd never do anything to hurt you."

"I know. And, I'll admit, I'm glad you explained things to me. There was a time in my life when I'd have been terrified, but this…" She trailed off with a little, bemused laugh. "Don't ever stop."

He hugged her tightly again. "Good. But I do have to warn you. I know of a clamp that spreads your pussy lips with a ring on the bar running through the middle that will suit my desires just as much as piercing you without causing you pain."

Alizay chuckled. "Of course you do. Doesn't surprise me in the least."

"Come on. Let's go upstairs and do this again. Only this time, I'm gonna take my time. Drive you fuckin' crazy."

"You already do, but I'm game. Just a suggestion. You might want to pull up your pants. Much as I like the view, I think I'd be a bit jealous of other women ogling you."

Blood gave her a gentle kiss, sweeping his tongue into her mouth, making her want him all over again. "I'd be disappointed if you weren't."

Alizay straightened her own clothing, readying to make a dash up to their room so they could continue. The grin he shot her was positively wicked, and she could only imagine what he had planned. And if he really did have a clamp like he described…

He'd just taken her hand when his phone buzzed. "Fuck," he swore softly, pulling out the device. Taking a quick peek, he started to put it back in his pocket, then did a double take. "Mother fuck!" His hand tightened on hers painfully. "Go to your room, Alizay. Go now and lock the door." Blood started to dash out of the gym, but Alizay gripped his hand.

"What's happened?"

"We've got company. Cain and Thorn have called for all hands on deck. Preferably armed."

"I'm not hiding like a child, Blood. Cain made me part of ExFil. You don't honestly think he didn't teach me to fight and handle a gun, did you?"

Blood looked at her, a grin tugging at the corner of his mouth despite the gravity of the situation as he saw it and his obvious need to get back to his brothers. "You and I are gonna have a fuckin' good life together."

Chapter Nine

Blood snagged two guns from the stash he'd hidden in the gym when he'd first arrived at the Demon mansion. Not that he didn't trust his hosts, he just believed in being prepared. Now, he was plenty glad of it. He handed Alizay one of the two Sig Saurs and two full clips. She checked her weapon, slid in a clip, and chambered a round like a pro. Blood grinned and did the same. His phone buzzed again, prompting another glance.

"Thorn says we've got guests of the uninvited sort. Apparently, Magenta's father, El Diablo, has brought a contingent of Black Reign with him." He frowned as he read the next text that popped up. "And several young women? What the fuck?"

"I thought this was a family gathering of the clubs? You said the club girls didn't come with you. Only ol' ladies and serious girlfriends."

"That was the plan. Christmas here when they weren't sure how I'd progress -- cause I'm such a popular guy and all -- then Christmas at home for everyone."

They made their way back to the great room where the decorating and eating and partying were going on. The room was silent, the men in full protective mode, pushing their women and the children into a circle of protection as the group headed by El Diablo from Black Reign stood at the front entrance.

"I'm not sure whether to be offended or flattered." El Diablo stood at the head of his group, hands at his sides in a non-threatening gesture. He was dressed immaculately in a three-piece suit, glittering cufflinks, rings, and a big-ass, expensive-looking watch. Definitely more of a fit with Shadow Demons than either Salvation's Bane or Bones.

"How about 'be gone?'" Cain stepped forward slightly, his own Sig at the ready. "This is a private party."

"I understand," El Diablo said, still holding his pose. His men hadn't moved, but one of the women wiggled between the men and let out a glad cry as she dashed for Lucy, Vicious's woman.

"Mae!" Lucy met her halfway, despite Vicious's mad grab for her. The chaplain of Salvation's Bane put himself between his woman and the Black Reign men, backing the women toward the combined group of Bones and Bane men.

El Diablo smiled. "Contrary to what you might think, we were invited to a family get together." As he said that, a more sedate pair of women crept from the Black Reign group.

"Serelda?" Darcy, Viper's woman, gasped. "Winter!" She, too, tried to dart forward, but Viper was ready and managed to keep her in the circle of their protection.

"I know, lil' bit. I know. But let them come to you." The two women hurried to Darcy, and the three embraced. Blood knew little about the history, but he knew Winter and Serelda were Darcy's stepsisters. Rayburn, the girl's father and Darcy's stepfather, had abused them and tried to sell them into sexual slavery. While Darcy had gotten away and ran before he could assault her, Winter and Serelda weren't so lucky. In the end, Winter had stabbed Rayburn to death in the Bones church. The girls had then gone with a man from Black Reign, El Diablo's personal guard. A man they called The Reaper. El Segador.

Thorn looked like he was about to lay into El Diablo when Alexi and Azriel of the Shadow Demons entered the room behind Black Reign. "Relax, guys. We invited him."

"Why the fuck would you do that?" Cain's gaze was hard, his expression like granite.

"Because El Diablo has been instrumental in tracking down our terrorists. He only wanted an invite to the decorating party so he could talk with his daughter."

"He did?" Magenta, Sword's woman and El Diablo's daughter, asked her question almost shyly.

"Absolutely, my dear." El Diablo dropped his hands to his sides. "I've missed so much of your life, when I found out about your... condition, I had to see you in person." He managed to look both contrite and happy at the same time. "Forgive me?"

"Daddy," she whispered. Tears swam in her eyes, and her hands automatically went to her belly. Sword looked like he wanted to throttle El Diablo, but restrained himself in favor of wrapping his wife in his big arms to let her gather her composure.

"I also wanted to come for another reason." El Diablo moved slowly toward Cain and Thorn, who stood at the head of the group in front of the others. "I know Cain and I have our pasts, but I'd like for you to know that after I examined the true relationship between ExFil and Bones, I realized the tight bond you had with your men. I never seriously considered a takeover after that. Stunner was never really in place to spy on you. I knew of the children he risked his life to help and wanted to let him be their guardian as he saw fit." He gave a repentant grin, as if he simply couldn't help himself. "Sadly, I have a reputation to uphold. Had I not continued with the guise of wanting a man on the inside to learn all your secrets, my men might have thought me weak and unable to lead them. In truth, I wanted to nurture your organizations in the hopes we could benefit each other in the future."

Cain crossed his arms over his chest and glanced at Thorn who simply shrugged. "A pretty speech. Doesn't make it true."

"I can only offer you my word." He smiled that shark-like grin once more. "Well, that, and all my considerable resources and contacts. I imagine ExFil could use a little hand when out of the country."

"How can you help us?" Cain ask suspiciously.

El Diablo shrugged. "Think of it as the Force. You walk in the light. I walk on the dark side. One without the other is powerful, but in order to get maximum benefits, you need to embrace both. I have contacts with the people you worry about overseas and can guarantee they're more afraid of me than they are defiant of you. They might still push you, but they will most likely keep a healthy distance."

Cain raised an eyebrow. "That's... a powerful offer. You'll understand if I'm skeptical. And by the way. Bitter much?"

"I can probably shed some light on that." Azriel stepped forward looking every bit as smart in his own expensive suit as El Diablo did. "You remember the chat we all had when Zora was in danger?"

"Yeah. Data still worries over that discussion. Still not sure he's convinced the Brotherhood intends to leave her alone."

"I'm not," Data confirmed. "What does that have to do with this?"

"Remember, it all stops with the Brotherhood." El Diablo brought their attention back to him. "I may not be part of them anymore, but I still have their contacts. I still police their assassins to keep innocents from being wrongfully killed." He gave them another dazzling grin. "I'm actually quite a big deal."

"I give you my word, Cain," Azriel said solemnly. "I wouldn't put your club or, more importantly, your women and children in danger. Not for any reason."

Cain and Thorn looked at each other for a long time. Finally, Thorn nodded once. Cain spread his hands in welcome. "Why the fuck not? It's Christmas, after all. Join us. But I have to warn you. The kids love glitter. You don't want your expensive duds gettin' all decorated, then change. Declining to be decorated is not an option."

Things went smoothly after that. Magenta did cry, but they were tears of joy. El Diablo's eyes looked suspiciously damp, but he simply didn't acknowledge it and hid any emotion with his usual superior attitude and cocky grin. The family reunions went well, and the three young women from Black Reign made some new friends. Stunner even dressed up as Santa, even though it was still three weeks before Christmas. The children from the Shadow Demons' household loved Santa, even though he didn't talk much. Through it all, Alizay looked on from a distance with a little grin.

"You should mingle," Blood said, resting his hands on her shoulders and squeezing gently. "Might be the last time you get to for a while."

She looked back over her shoulder and gave him a small but content smile. "I'm good. I like watching. Besides, it's still a little overwhelming."

"Maybe I could persuade you to come to bed, then." He said it close to her ear, hoping to see her delicate skin erupt in goose flesh. He wasn't disappointed.

"That's the best idea I've heard all day."

They made it to Alizay's room without a detour. This time, Blood was able to take appreciate her body the way he wanted to. As he stripped her, he marveled again at the perfection he had in his arms. She was lithe muscle and smooth, soft skin wrapped in a powder keg of passion. When she made love with him, Alizay threw everything she was into it, enjoying every second to the fullest. It was a wonder she could. Blood knew that he'd never take her for granted and he'd always do everything he could to make sex exciting for her. "Have I told you how very beautiful you are, Alizay?"

She smiled shyly at him. "I'm not sure. But you could tell me again."

He chuckled. "You are. So very beautiful."

They kissed and clung to each other. Somehow, Blood managed to rid himself of his clothes before crawling after her into bed. Framing her head with his forearms as he entered her slowly, Blood studied every expression crossing her face, needing to watch the passion blossom within her. "That's my girl," he whispered. "Take me inside you."

"Blood..." She threaded her fingers through his hair and pulled him down to kiss her as he moved slowly in and out of her wet little pussy. Alizay wrapped her legs around him, not urging him faster, but simply hugging him to her. She met his thrusts with her own, always following his lead, apparently content to drag the moment out before they both lost themselves in each other.

"If I live to be a hundred, I'll never get enough of you, Alizay."

"Me neither," she said grinning up at him. "I never knew it could be like this."

"It will only get better, baby." With that, he shifted his body, changing his angle and hooking her thigh higher over his hip. The change in position was exactly what Alizay needed. Her eyes widened, and her mouth formed a silent "O" of surprise. Blood picked up the pace, riding her harder and harder with every stroke. Their breathing became erratic and loud in the room. Sweat broke out over Blood's skin, and he threw his head back just as Alizay screamed his name. Her cunt squeezed around him as she came, milking him of his seed. He gladly gave it to her in a fiery explosion that had him seeing stars.

Blood gasped as he pulled her to him, rolling to his back. Alizay lay on top of him, her body still filled with his cock. Neither of them spoke. Blood stroked her back up and down, needing to touch her to calm himself. She settled his heart and mind like nothing else ever had. He supposed that she'd strengthened more than just his body with her therapy. She'd strengthened his spirit. He found in himself something he hadn't even realized he was missing. Now, every part of him was filled with her. His Alizay. *His love.*

"I know I've not said it before," he began, clearing his throat. Emotion wasn't his strong suit. "But I love you, Alizay. Ain't never told a woman that before."

She pushed up to look at him, her brows drawn together. "Don't fuck with me, Blood. You don't have to say it if you don't mean it. I know it will come because I can feel it, too, but you don't have to say it yet."

"Baby, you should know by now I don't say nothin' I don't mean, so I want you to understand me here. I. Love. You."

Alizay looked at him for a long time. She searched for something as she studied him. Blood could only give her the truth. He truly did love her.

Finally, after several long moments, she smiled. "I love you, too."

"When we get back to Florida, I'll have you a property patch made. When you're ready, you can wear it and it will be official. But you take your time. Really think about it. 'Cause once you put it on, it's done. You'll be mine forever."

"I don't need to think about it, Blood. I think I've known since the moment I saw you."

"I was so fucked up, that stupid body armor stuck wrong. Then you leaned over me, the sun shining behind you like a halo. I knew then I was a goner."

"You were pretty fucked up," she said, grinning at his disgruntled look. "I saw how brave you were, getting that family off the street and to shelter. If anyone deserved help, it was you. Then when I learned your other hip hadn't been properly rehabilitated, I knew I had to try to fix it. I wanted to see you whole and strong, like the warrior I knew you were."

"You worked a miracle. I'm in the best shape of my life, and my hip has never felt this good. Hell, I think I'm stronger than I was before either injury. Thanks to you."

"I can't take that credit. You put in the work. I just kept you motivated."

"Maybe so, but it's your spirit that filled all the holes inside me. Sounds cheesy as fuck, but you're the other half of my soul, Alizay. The best half."

When she leaned in to kiss him, Blood tasted tears as one silently trickled down her cheek. He kissed it from her skin before going back to her mouth. He kissed her for a long, long time, simply enjoying the ability to do so.

When he finally let her up for air, she sighed contentedly. "I love you. I love you so much, Blood."

"I love you too, baby. Merry Christmas."

She giggled. "Best. Christmas. Ever."

Stryker (Salvation's Bane MC 6)

Marteeka Karland

Glitter: Yes, that's my real name. A born stripper name, I know. I've been on my own since I was 14. When I tried to get a job with Salvation's Bane MC as a stripper at their club, Salvation's Angels, their security saw right through my fake ID. Lucky for me, the club sent me to Beach Fit, their fitness club, until I turned 18. Now I work at Angels, and the crowd here loves me. Stryker's still looking out for me. For some reason he thinks I'm a magnet for trouble. Now that I've got his full attention, I'm going to prove him right. I know what I want, and I'm going to prove him right.

Stryker: We try our best to keep things at the club legit. Last thing we need is an underage dancer attracting too much attention. OK, so she's legal now, has been for nearly two years, but that girl's everything this old man doesn't need -- and can't afford.

There's another club encroaching on our territory, setting up a BDSM club on the other side of town -- as a front to run drugs. Now I've got word there's even more going on at The Dark than just drugs. I was right. And who do I find right in the middle of it but Glitter. Only, she's not involved with the thugs at The Dark. She's their prisoner -- a sub who has no idea what it means to be a sub, but she thinks she wants to learn.

Challenge issued? Challenge 'effin accepted.

Chapter One

There was no possible way for Stryker to ignore the little pixie dancer twirling around the pole half naked. He'd been watching her every fucking night she'd worked for a couple of months now, unable to take his focus someplace else. Glitter was not a woman he'd normally pursue. She was too innocent for the likes of him. He'd known it from the moment she plopped herself down in the chair across from his desk and told him her name was Glitter. And that, yes, that was her real name. Laugh at his own peril.

But here he was. Prowling the main room at Salvation's Angels instead of checking on things over at the Playground. So he could watch Glitter's set. Or, more accurately, so he could watch Glitter. Period.

The girl haunted his dreams. She wasn't what one would call a classic beauty, but she had a force of personality that everyone she met loved and wanted to soak up. When she danced on stage, she was a temptress. When she played off stage, she was like a little kitten. Stryker wasn't normally attracted to the bubbly type, but Glitter was more than just her personality. He had no idea why, but underneath the sex appeal he sensed a vulnerable woman. There were times when Stryker could see her scanning the room when she thought no one was watching and she just looked... tired. Especially when she had to mediate one squabble or another with the girls in the dressing room. It was that vulnerability that fascinated Stryker and made him want Glitter with everything in him.

Well, tonight he was going to have her. He was a patched member of Salvation's Bane, and she was an employee at Salvation's Angels. They weren't supposed to fraternize with each other, but Stryker wasn't above bending a few rules. Thorn might kick his ass if he found out he'd fucked the bubbly little dancer, but it would be worth it. And any man who wouldn't risk the wrath of his president to sample a woman didn't want to taste her bad enough.

Finally, Glitter sashayed her sweet ass out onto the stage in front of the long runway. She was dressed as a naughty kitten, complete with a long, silky tail she twirled when she walked. When she turned around, she made the fucking thing dance as she shook her ass and snapped her hips back and forth like a belly dancer. As always, she had the crowd mesmerized with sexual electricity.

As she revealed inch after inch of creamy, lightly freckled skin, Stryker became wound tighter and tighter. He wanted her. Wanted her with a fierce passion that bordered on the insane. The mere fact that other men were watching from the floor below her nearly put him in a killing rage because they coveted what he considered his. Which was insane, because he would never let any woman of his work in a place like this. Not because he thought it was beneath her. On the contrary. He was proud of her. She was the most beautiful, most desirable woman there, and she should be proud to show everyone how truly gorgeous her body was. No. He'd never let her work here because he was a jealous son of a bitch. While he had no problem showing off his woman in public, he needed to be at her side when she stood there naked. Every man in the fucking place might know they could look, but he'd kill anyone who even thought about touching.

He watched Glitter as she danced, twirling around on the poles, spinning upside down in only the garter that held her tips. Her thong had long since come off. God! The things he could do to that lithe little body of hers! He'd fantasized about so many things since the first day he'd laid eyes on her. When he finally fucked her, it was going to take days to explore everything he'd imagined. Weeks even.

They were on the second of three tiers in Salvation's Angels. Glitter always worked tier two. Occasionally she allowed a patron to take her to tier three for a lap dance, but it was rare. In fact, he'd only known of two times she'd done it. Both times the money she'd turned in as the house's take had been astronomical.

The first tier of the club was like any other strip joint. The women kept on their thongs and generally went about topless the whole time. Lap dances were closely monitored, and the hands-off rule was strictly followed. Tier two was for patrons who were willing to pay more for admission, and dollar bills were swapped in favor of tens. But the girls were nude, there wasn't an enforced hands-off policy on that tier. The girls didn't have to allow touching if they didn't want to be, but most of them enjoyed the interaction, and those who didn't usually worked the first tier anyway.

The third tier was where the more uncensored lap dances were bought. Penetration was prohibited, but there had been more than one woman who'd allowed things to go further than strictly allowed. As manager of the club, Stryker gave the girls on this tier free rein. If they wanted to let their patron pay them for sex, who was he to stop it? As long as it was consensual and no one went blabbing to the cops, he couldn't give two fucks. And the patrons paid enough for the privilege of being on that third floor that he knew they weren't going to go to the cops. Any who might… well. They didn't get as far as the second tier. The only hard and fast rule was that members of

Salvation's Bane were off limits. Not that the brothers would immediately claim a woman they'd fucked, but the Angels were a huge draw. If word got out there were brawls over women, they'd lose the wealthier clients who wouldn't take kindly to the police raiding them every fucking night.

Tonight, Stryker decided he was going to take advantage of his role as manager and boss of the club. Maybe he wouldn't get Glitter to let him fuck her, but he was getting a lap dance, and it would likely keep him awake at night with a horrible case of blue balls for a very long time.

The thought had just entered his head when Glitter spotted him. Her gaze slid over him once before darting back. She gave him a huge smile before continuing her dance. She'd join him the second she got off stage. Glitter wasn't one to throw herself at men, she was just a touchy-feely kind of person. She considered all the men from Bane her very best friends, since she couldn't date any of them. But she always, always, made a point to welcome Stryker with open arms and a big bear hug any time she saw him. As much as a pint-sized pixie could bear-hug, at least.

By the end of her song, Glitter had bills stuffed in the sparkling band around her waist. Stryker noticed that her thong had ended up draped over the head of an admirer closer to the stage. She blew kisses as she sauntered backstage to store the tips. It was never long before she made her way back to the floor. Sure enough, it was just a few minutes before she came trotting out from the dressing room to the main floor, naked as the day she was born, and made a beeline straight to Stryker, jumping into his arms with a squeal. Like always, she wrapped her arms and legs around him tightly, as if it had been years since she'd seen him. Of course, she often did the same to several of the bouncers and security at Angels. She said it was her thanks for them keeping her safe. "I missed you so much!" She squeezed so hard, Stryker believed she really had missed him.

He laughed. "Missed you, too, baby."

She gave him one final squeeze before kissing his cheek and unwinding herself to slide to the floor. "You see my dance?"

"Do I ever miss your dances?"

She smiled brightly. "Never."

"I didn't miss it tonight, either." He took her arm, pulling her closer to him so he could wrap his arm around her shoulder. "Need a favor tonight."

"You name it, and it's yours!"

Oh, that sweet, gullible face… Stryker almost felt bad for what he was about to do. Almost. He was just bastard enough to not give a damn how much he was pressing his luck with her. She was a big girl. If she wanted to say no, she would.

"I need a dance."

She grinned. "That's easy."

"A lap dance. Upstairs."

Glitter tilted her head as if confused, then her eyes widened and she grinned. "You have a special friend? You know I'll make it worth his time. Come on!" She took his hand and headed for the stairs. As they moved, she looked around her, raising her voice to be heard over the music and cheers of patrons as the girls lost their clothing. "Where is he?"

"Just keep moving." Stryker urged her forward, taking the lead as they trotted up the stairs. He couldn't help but watch her. Her tits were small, but they still moved lusciously as she skipped up one step after another. It was all Stryker could do not to groan in frustration. This was either going to be a serious mistake, or the best decision he'd ever made in his life.

He led her to a back corner, as far away from everyone as he could. It was an area most people never made it to because it was at the opposite end of the entrance and most of the guys brought up here didn't want to wait long enough to walk that far. Stryker knew it would be worth it.

Each cubby had its own sofa or love seat. Some of the cubbies were larger and had more room for the woman to dance, though most of the time, lead ups weren't needed. Everything was over in the space of one song unless the patron paid for another. Stryker wanted this to be different. Maybe not necessarily longer, but he wanted Glitter to lose herself in this.

"Wait here," he instructed her. He moved the sofa out of the way. There was nothing soft about what Stryker wanted with Glitter. When she wrapped her body around him, there was going to be no give to anything. He returned with a steel folding chair, plopped it down, then sprawled out in it.

"I… don't get it," she said, looking adorably confused. "You want me to dance. For you?"

"I do. And I want your full attention."

Glitter was silent for a long time, crossing her arms over her chest and glancing toward the camera. She looked hurt. "Are you testing me? Because I know the rules, Stryker. No dancing with the club members. No single dances on the floor. No lap dances anywhere."

Ah. That made sense. She was worried he didn't trust her. "Not testing you, honey. Just wanna see what you got." He gave her what he hoped was a lascivious, challenging smile. "Only two times you came up here you brought in more money than ten dancers."

"You've been keeping tabs on me?" She cocked her slender hip out, resting a hand there. "Look. I choose not to come up here very often. It's too..." She waved her hand around. "I don't know. Intimate? Just a man and a woman. Grinding. Gyrating." She suddenly got a wicked gleam in her eye and grinned at him. "Then again, maybe that's exactly what you've been wanting?"

The little witch knew him well. Not surprising. She seemed to know all the men's quirks and how best to soothe them when they became riled for whatever reason. Why Stryker thought he would be any different, he didn't know.

"I suppose it is," he said, spreading out his arms. "Impress me. I'll pay well for the dance. Or dances."

Music from the club below was loud around them. Stryker watched in rapt fascination as Glitter's expression changed from the sweet girl he'd come to know into a sex goddess right before his eyes.

She was naked already. Even the little elaborate elastic belt decorated with gems and sequins she sometimes wore around her waist to hold her tips was gone. He wasn't certain when she'd lost it, but she stood before him, glittering jewelry dangling from her nipples, her little navel piercing winking at him, and dangling chains with gemstones dangling from her bare little pussy. Her body shifted and swayed in an elegant display of grace and sensuality.

"How about I just dance," she purred, running her hands over her body, flicking the gems at her nipples so they swayed and glistened in the dim lighting. "You want a show or the full package?"

"Give me everything, baby. Don't hold back anything. I'll pay you well."

She shrugged one delicate shoulder. "Ain't worried 'bout the money, sugar. Just relax and enjoy yourself. I'll take care of the rest."

And put on a show she did. She danced teasingly, avoiding touching him too much, but occasionally bending down to grab his face in her delicate hands and sigh as she brushed her face against his. Her breasts scraped tantalizingly against him when she did, and it wasn't long before she'd pulled his T-shirt off and let her body, shimmering with a lotion that made her skin smell heavenly and feel as soft as silk, brush his naked torso as she worked her magic.

It seemed like she was waiting for the right song. Finally a hard, driving metal song started, with heavy guitars buzzing and bass pounding. She straddled him, seating herself fully on his lap with her legs spread wide.

Glitter took advantage of her surroundings. The chair made her able to come in full contact with Stryker. Her legs draped over his so that she almost touched the floor with her shoes. She shimmied her hips so that she rubbed over his cock in a circular motion that was slowly but surely driving him fucking mad with wanting her. His cock strained his jeans, and there was no way she could not feel how she affected him.

Stryker laid his hands gently on her hips, caressing her ass as she moved on him. She was so fucking soft! His hands wandered up her sides and then back to her ass. Her thighs. All the while she ground herself against him, her breaths coming in little pants. Glitter threaded her fingers through his hair, fisting them as she brought her face to his, mere inches from his lips. Occasionally, she moaned and flicked her tongue out to lap at her own lips.

"Feel good?" He asked the question on impulse. She'd gone into something like a trance, and Stryker couldn't imagine she wasn't loving what she was doing to him.

"Makes me want to come," she whispered against his lips. "Your big, hard cock is right there. Just waiting for me to let him out. I bet he wants inside me, doesn't he?"

"Abso-fuckin'-lutely," he gasped out as she pressed down on him, dragging her cunt over his cock in a hard, searing drag.

"I'd probably come the second you got inside me," she said, panting. "Would you want my pussy or my little asshole?"

"Who said I'd have to choose?" Stryker was losing it. He was seconds away from putting her words into action. His hand snaked around her, pulling her little body closer to him as he ran his middle finger down the seam of her ass only to find her plugged. He sucked in a breath and she giggled.

To his utter displeasure, she stood, swinging her leg over his lap, and turned around in front of him, bending over at the waist and looking up at him from between her legs. Her fingers fondled her pussy, which was dripping wet, and reached further back to caress the crown of a fiery red stone on the head of the plug in her ass.

She scissored the adornment between her fingers and pulled it partly out of her ass before pushing it back in again. "Would you want to remove the plug? Or simply slide in beside it?"

"Fuck, woman!"

He reached for her, pulling her back so she sat back on his lap. Stryker yanked her knees apart, his hand shooting out to smack her pussy with three hard slaps. Glitter cried out, arching her back, thrusting her breasts up beautifully. With his other hand, Stryker cupped one breast, pulling at the adornments on her nipple until the tight little bud stretched outward.

"Greedy little thing, aren't you?"

"Only with you," she whispered. Stryker found her clit and, fingers wet with her juices, circled it with one finger. Seconds later, Glitter screamed, shuddering in his arms. Stryker thrust his hips against her ass, rubbing and grinding until he found his own release. Creaming his pants. Fuck.

Fuck!

Glitter sagged against him, sweat slickening her skin. Stryker wrapped his arms around her, breathing just as hard as she was. The afterglow lasted only a moment. Glitter stiffened, then sucked in a breath. She stood abruptly. When she turned around, she had a jubilant smile on her face.

"That was awesome, Stryker."

"It certainly was," he said, digging into his pocket. Glitter's eyes got big and round and she backed up, raising her hands as if to fend him off.

"No, no. That was on the house. Just pay the house take at the bar."

"You earned this, Glitter."

Did he imagine the sheen of tears on her face? If so, her smile told a different story. "Nope. I insist. See you next time." She blew him a little kiss before hurrying out of the room. Before he could get his legs under him and sprint after her, Glitter had vanished in the dimly lit area. Probably back to the dressing room.

No matter. He'd wait for her in the parking lot. He knew her vehicle. Once he had her out of the club and alone, he'd get her on his bike and back to his house. He'd work out things with Thorn later, but little Glitter was his. One way or another.

Chapter Two

That was the stupidest thing she'd ever done. Glitter knew better. She knew not to put anything to do with sex between her and any member of Salvation's Bane. She'd worked for Salvation's Angels longer than anyone currently at the club. More than four years. She'd come to them when she was sixteen. Had lied about her age. Which lasted all of fifteen minutes before Justice had found her out. Thorn had given her a stern talking to, then put her to work at Beach Fit, a fitness club the MC owned, and a lease on one of the houses Salvation's Bane owned but didn't use. For that, Glitter would be forever grateful. She owed her life to the club. That was a debt she could never repay.

As she trotted downstairs to the second-tier dressing room, she was more than a little ashamed of herself. It wasn't that she'd gotten off dancing for a guy, but that the guy had been Stryker. Not just a patched member of Salvation's Bane, but the freaking head of security at the Playground. She'd broken the rules and done it in high fashion. It didn't matter that he'd wanted her to, or even told her to. Glitter never broke the rules. Not like this. The rules against club members and dancers mixing were in place for everyone's sanity. Glitter had developed friendships with all the Bane members who frequented the club, but had never crossed the line like this. But, of course, she'd do it with Stryker.

Glitter had loved Stryker from the day they'd first met. He was so larger than life, if a bit surly, she had no defense against him. She was far from the star-struck teenager she'd been the first time she'd met him, but she always felt that same thrill when she was in the same room interacting with him. This encounter had been off the charts.

He'd been masterful, just a hint showing through of the dominant she knew him to be. He'd commanded her body and her mind. Made her want to please him in every way she could. Just that lift of his eyebrow when he'd told her to dance for him had been her undoing. She'd always craved a dominant lover, but even the short time it had taken to get them both off had shown her Stryker was exactly the type of man she needed. Only he was off limits.

She showered quickly, getting as much of the glitter and the shimmery lotions and oils off her skin as she could. Technically, she had another two hours, but there was no way she could go back there tonight. The floor was covered with more than enough girls, and Glitter had done her one stage set tonight. She had to get out of there before she had a panic attack.

"Where you going, Glitter?" Tanya, one of the dancers, nearly ran into Glitter as she opened the door coming back inside after a break. Likely the woman was getting a hit of her drug of the week.

"Something came up. I'm done for the night anyway."

"I was gonna ask you to take my stage slot." The other woman glanced around them as if looking for someone. "I got a quota to meet or my ass is grass."

"Quota?"

"Yeah." She pulled Glitter out the door and pushed it shut. "Listen. There's a new MC on the other side of town. They're picking up the smack and c-dust since Bane won't. Once they get set up here, they're gonna run Bane out." Glitter was horrified, but Tanya kept going. "I got a bunch of stuff I need to get out there." She giggled. "Or I might use it myself." She continued to giggle. When Glitter just looked at her, she let out a nervous breath. "Seriously though. They just want to get their product out there for people to know someone new's in town."

"You can't be pushing drugs here, Tanya. Stryker and Thorn won't tolerate it. You know the rules."

"Yeah, well, I ain't pushin' 'em here, am I?" Tanya snapped at Glitter as she lit a joint and took a long pull. "Look, I just need some extra time tonight. Take my time. It's close to the end of the night. The tips will be great." They wouldn't. By the time Tanya took the stage most everyone was spent out. She was new so she had to start at the bottom and work her way up.

"I can't, Tanya. I took your time two nights ago. I have my own problems."

The girl huffed smoke in Glitter's face. The sharp, "skunk" smell made Glitter want to gag, but she held her expression while waving her hand in front of her face. "Of course you do. Everyone always says if you need anything, go see Glitter. The one time I come to you, you won't even listen to me."

"I worked for you just last week. And the week before that. You always have someplace better to be. If you think I'm the only one who notices, you're wrong. You don't pick up the pace, you'll be gone."

"You threatenin' me?"

"Just telling you the facts." Glitter snatched the joint from Tanya and tossed it to the ground, stomping it with her foot.

"Hey! Bitch!"

"Either get to work or go home, Tanya. No one is going to cover for you anymore. We're all here to make money. Us. The club. Even the bartenders and the DJ. You think you need more than you're getting now, talk to Havoc. He's the boss."

"Yeah, well, fuck you, Glitter!"

Glitter didn't respond. She hurried to her car and left the parking lot wondering what to do next. She felt strung out. Exhausted. She loved working at Salvation's Angels, but the whole thing was weighing on her. Probably because she wanted Stryker so bad and knew she'd never be able to have him as long as she worked in the strip club. If she quit, she had no means of supporting herself. She had no education. No marketable skills. She was a stripper. Pure and simple.

She needed relief from all this. The guilt. The frustration. She needed a Dom to punish her, then take care of her. To help her love herself again. Pathetic? Probably. But there it was.

Normally, she'd have gone to Miami and the Fetish Factory. But it was late. She didn't want to drive that far and didn't want to spend any of tonight's earnings on something as frivolous as a hotel after an hour or so of playing.

While Bane owned the local BDSM club, the Playground, there was another recently opened club on the other side of town. They called it the Dark. From what Glitter had heard, the place was a bit on the hardcore side of things, but she hadn't heard anything negative. Admittedly, she was new to the scene. Had actually only watched most of the time, participating in only one or two light scenes. She knew enough to know she needed to check out a club before she actually played, but tonight, she needed more than being a voyeur.

Decision made, she headed to the Dark. She'd start out watching. If she met someone who caught her fancy, she'd try playing a little. She certainly wasn't into too much pain, but a little spanking as punishment for her deeds tonight might be freeing. Relieve some of the guilt, maybe. Time would tell. The knots in her chest and stomach weren't going away on their own. If this didn't work, she'd simply go to Havoc and confess her sins. Probably should anyway, but no sense in causing trouble if she could come to terms with it. God knew she'd learned her lesson. Never again would she be alone with Stryker. Never.

* * *

Moans and cries followed sharp smacks in the dark of the club's interior. The Playground was almost in a frenzy tonight. It was like the full moon possessed everyone with a membership and they just had to be out to get their freak on. Stryker had been called in because club security had their hands full. It had taken exactly ten minutes to calm everyone down. Not because his men weren't good at their jobs. Stryker was just that fucking mean. Things were going well enough he might be able to leave in an hour or so. After checking in on things at Angels, and the dance with Glitter followed by her sudden disappearance, Stryker had hoped he could find some willing sub to take the edge off. No such luck.

Just as well. He needed to check on the club on the other side of town. It was opened by some shady characters, and there were rumors the prostitutes weren't all willing. Stryker loved a good roll in the hay with an experienced woman just as much as the next guy, and he didn't mind paying well for his particular kinks, nor would he judge a woman for charging him. But he could not stand by and let a woman be raped so her pimp could get paid. He'd discussed the possibility with Thorn, the president of Salvation's Bane, and they'd agreed Stryker would stake out the situation.

"You headed out?" Tobias was his right hand while Stryker was Tobias's left hand. They'd worked together so long each knew the other's moods on sight.

"Checkin' out the new club across town."

"Yeah. Heard you might be headed that way."

Stryker stalked through the crowd, not even glancing to see if Tobias had stayed behind. He knew the fucker wouldn't. Stryker intended on doing this by himself. Mainly because he was looking for Glitter. The little vixen thought she was doing something in secret. Fortunately, most of the girls loved her. She hadn't said much, but one of them had said she'd been asking about the new club. The Dark, it was called. Apparently, she'd left with the thought she might check it out. Stryker knew she went out of town from time to time to watch at another BDSM club. He'd had even followed to make sure nothing happened to her. He'd never interfered because she'd seemed curious. But, if she was at the Dark, that stopped tonight. If he got the notion, he'd decided he might just take down the fuckin' club out of principle. This was Salvation's Bane territory. Another club did not set up shop in their backyard without permission. That included motherfuckers who thought they could hurt women and give MCs a bad name all at the same time. And if any of them got it in their head to hurt Glitter, he'd make death slow and painful.

As he straddled his big Harley, he glanced at Tobias, who was doing the same. "Don't need you on this one."

"Never said you did." Tobias gave him a lopsided grin and started up his bike. The roar of the pipes guaranteed Stryker couldn't get the last word. Instead, he started his own bike and took off.

The new club was across town, about thirty minutes away with traffic. Stryker used the time to think about what he hoped to accomplish. Riding down the highway with the wind in his face and the bike roaring between his legs was the only way he could calm himself enough to think about this.

The Dark was rumored to be run by an MC, but no one seemed to know who. Even Data at Bones, Bane's sister club, couldn't find it. He'd be glad when Justice got out of prison. The man might not be good on the computer shit like Data, but he had ways of knowing everything there was to know about Palm Beach. Still, the mere fact Data hadn't been able to dig something up made Stryker suspect it had something to do with that fucking El Diablo.

The man was a thorn in everyone's side. Since Bones was a good thirteen or so hours away, El Diablo only harassed them occasionally. But he and his club, Black Reign, were nipping at the heels of Salvation's Bane on a daily basis. Bane was situated in Palm Beach, while Reign was firmly planted in Lake Worth. They'd never known Black Reign to willfully hurt women since El Diablo had taken over, though. Perhaps they'd simply overlooked it.

"Goddamn motherfucker," he muttered under his breath.

Stryker didn't have to glance to his left to know Tobias was pulling up beside him, putting himself on the inside and in the most danger from traffic in the other lane. They often did that for each other when one of them was distracted. Tobias didn't glance at Stryker. Just kept riding like normal. It was an annoyance that the other man felt he had to baby-sit, but it was also a relief to know someone had his back. If Black Reign did own the Dark, it meant he would definitely need backup. It would also mean the club was upping its game. Which meant El Diablo would have to be dealt with now. If Black Reign wasn't involved, then Bane had to find out who owned the club and what their game was. Either way, Thorn needed to know so he could decide how to proceed next.

They rolled into the parking lot of the Dark, right up to the front fucking door. And, yes, Glitter's little Fusion was parked at in the back under a light. At least she took care of her safety.

Just outside the entrance, bouncer looking on warily, Stryker revved his big Hog several times. A challenge. He didn't do subtle. There might be only two of them, but they could make their presence known and send a message without causing a war. If they wanted to. In any case, he was here to look. Not crush. If it was, indeed, Black Reign who owned the club, they'd know pretty soon after entering. Even if El Diablo wanted to stay on the down low, he wouldn't continue with a charade once it was discovered. He might not come clean with what he was doing, but he'd acknowledge he was in charge. It was just the way he operated.

Once inside, however, Stryker was certain El Diablo and Black Reign had nothing to do with what he was seeing. El Diablo was diabolical and more than a little sinister and kinky, but this place bordered on the depraved. Even for Stryker's tastes.

Scattered all over the massive main room were cages filled with up to four women. Some looked willing to be there. Others did not. All of them were naked. Men stood around them in various stages of undress, either masturbating until they came into the cage, or engaging in one sex act or another with the caged women. Some of the women had their legs through the bars spread wide so they could be fucked. Others sucked cock through the bars. Still others gave hand jobs. The ones who looked unwilling to participate were poked with what looked like cattle prods -- and quite likely were -- until they did as they were instructed. More than one that Stryker could see had circular buns over several areas of her body where she'd been shocked on multiple occasions. That was enough to give him pause, but what really bothered him were the women out of the cages.

A few were tied to St. Andrew's crosses, others suspended from the ceiling by their wrists while their feet dangled several inches above the floor, their ankles shackled so their legs were spread wide. Men with whips laid stripes over their flesh, some bringing blood with every lash.

"What the all-fired fuck?" Tobias was at his side, not any less horrified by what he was seeing than Stryker was.

"You got that right." Stryker didn't know what else to say.

"We can't leave these women here."

"I know." Stryker was stunned into inaction. It wasn't as if he hadn't seen worse, but always overseas in some God-forsaken third-world country or some shit. Not in his own Goddamned backyard.

"Who the fuck are you and how the fuck did you get the fuck in here?" The man who approached them looked like he might attempt to remove them by force. Or worse, simply kill them on the spot. Or, at least, he looked like he wanted to. Stryker could have told the guy that, in his present mood, it wasn't wise to challenge him.

"I'm the fuckin' bastard gonna take this fuckin' place down. Who the fuck are you? You own the joint?" Stryker advanced on the man. Though his opponent was larger, Stryker was meaner and more heavily muscled. This guy was a big-ass motherfucker, but he wasn't a fighter. He had a huge, square jaw that gave him a bruiser appearance, but his physique told a story of too much beer and not enough exercise. Likely the man was in this position because his looks and size easily intimidated.

The guy sneered. "You can try. Guarantee five men'll be here before you land the first punch."

Stryker's fist shot out and smashed into the guy's nose, spraying blood all over the place. "Really?" Stryker made a show of looking all around him before turning his full attention back on the man. "'Cause I don't see shit comin' to help you, motherfucker. Now who's in fucking charge?"

The guy spat at Stryker as blood dripped steadily from his nose down to his chin. "Fuck you."

The second the words were out of the guy's mouth, Stryker went low, stepping into the guy until he was looking straight into his eyes. His hand shot out and grabbed the guy's privates and squeezed without mercy. The guy let out a high-pitched squeal and Stryker maneuvered him against a nearby wall out of the flow of traffic and the dim lights.

"I'm gonna ask you one more time, Porky. Who's in fucking charge?"

"His name's Rat Man," Porky whimpered, sweat breaking out over his face as Stryker increased the pressure to his balls. "Owns the place, too."

"He belong to an MC?"

"Yeah. Outta Nashville, he says. Kiss of Death."

Stryker glanced at Tobias, who gave him a hard look before returning his attention to their surroundings. Kiss of Death was one of the worst clubs he knew. They were into all kinds of things from drugs to human trafficking. Mostly, they sold women, but had been known to sell children of both sexes. Angel had barely escaped them. Suzie, Cliff, and Daniel, too.

"He here?"

"Hell no! He spotted you guys and told me to make sure you had an accident before you left, and then he split."

"I want all these women released," Stryker said, tightening his grip once again. "Keys!" He held out his hand, but the bastard just shook his head.

"Ain't got 'em. Besides, every woman is here because she wants to be. I got contracts that say so."

"Don't look like some of them got what they signed up for," Tobias said, his voice soft and deadly. "Looks like more than a few would like to renegotiate their contracts."

"All they gotta do is say their safeword. Ain't no one here against their will."

"Then you won't mind us checkin'. Will ya." Stryker didn't make it a question. If his little menace was in here, he was going to tan her hide before he dragged her out on a fuckin' leash.

Stryker had no doubt Tobias had secured Porky somewhere, but it didn't take long for the other man to start quartering the room with Stryker. They went from woman to woman, in some cases having to physically restrain the men as they objected strenuously to them talking with the women. As they stormed through the crowd, pulling men away from their "submissives," activity around them gradually ceased. It didn't take long for them to garner the attention of security.

"I'm going to have to ask you to leave." The big, burly guy crossed his arms over a massive chest, an easy smirk on his face. Again, the guy had more bulk than muscle, but he held himself and moved like a guy who'd seen more than his fair share of action. Tobias saw it too. If he attacked, Tobias would go for the guy's knees and Stryker would go for the jugular a second later. It was the way they worked. One kill and anyone else thinking to take them on would think twice. If there was anything at all going on here other than consenting adults having fun, they wouldn't dare call the police.

"Ask all you want," Stryker said, moving to the next woman. So far, many of them had looked scared, but hadn't admitted to wanting to leave. Didn't mean they weren't intimidated into continuing, just meant they had to find one willing to trust them. Once that happened, the rest would follow.

The guy grabbed Stryker's arm. "Did you hear me, motherfu --"

Stryker snagged his wrist, pulling the guy into him and catching the guy's elbow. He pushed against the back of it with a hard, forceful thrust, hyperextending the joint. It snapped like a twig. Fucker wasn't stoic about the pain.

"You scream like a girl, motherfucker," Stryker said, bending close to his adversary, checking him for weapons. The two guns he found, Stryker removed, handing them to Tobias. Stryker kept the knife. "Now shut the fuck up before I shut you up."

Stryker moved on, still not finding a woman in the place willing to use her safeword, or just tell them to get her the fuck out of there. He was growing agitated, knowing this was wrong, when he spotted the one person he'd dreaded seeing.

Glitter was strung up by her wrists, a ball gag in her mouth. She was thrashing about, trying to scream above the music that was still blaring despite the disruption of activity throughout the club. The little pixie was a thorn in his side and his dick. Even before the sexual encounter earlier, he'd always admired Glitter. She was a sexy, sensual creature on stage. A feisty little punk off it. Now, she looked both pissed and afraid. He found he much preferred the former to the latter.

"What the fuck?" Tobias saw her, too.

"I know." Stryker stalked toward her and the soon-to-be-dead Dom who appeared to have claimed her, if the bright red collar around her neck was any indication. The Dom in question stepped between Stryker and Glitter as he and Tobias approached.

"She's mine," the man said. A hulking brute, he looked like he could readily break the much smaller woman in half.

"What is it with every motherfucking guy in this place?" Tobias muttered. "Bulk with no muscle. Bitch, I will beat you down with one hand."

This guy was bolder than the others. He stuck out his chest, bringing his whip to the ready. Stryker could tell he knew how to wield a whip just by the way he held it. Which told him Glitter was in way over her head. Having watched her for several months in the club she preferred, he knew she was in no way ready for something that hard core. He ignored the hulking beast in front of him.

"You good, Glitter?"

Immediately, she glanced at her tormentor. Just that little bit of hesitation when she knew Stryker would get her out of there without question. Thankfully, she shook her head several times, "no." Stryker immediately went to her, pulling the ball gag from her mouth.

"Get me down," she breathed, her voice barely above a whisper. The big man with her growled, but stepped back, allowing Stryker free access to Glitter. Good thing, because Stryker was ready and more than willing to kill. Glitter wasn't his woman, but she worked for him at his fucking club. Well, the club his MC owned. He was in charge of the security. Which made Glitter his to protect.

The second he got one wrist free, she was tugging at the second cuff, unbuckling it clumsily. Stryker wrapped one arm around her waist and used the other to bat her hand away and unbuckle the thing himself. He tried to set her on her feet, but her knees seemed to buckle. Tobias knelt and undid the cuffs on her ankles while Stryker kept a close eye on the people around them.

Once she was down, Glitter pushed away from him and went to a nearby bench. "Don't you leave, Stryker." She kept her eyes on him even as she snagged clothing. She didn't put anything on, just grabbed it and slipped her shoes on, her arms full of her belongings.

"Not plannin' on it, sweetheart."

"She's my sub," the big guy said. "I collared her."

"See that. Doesn't mean I'm ignoring her wishes."

"Glitter," the guy said menacingly.

She didn't say anything, but stared at him wide-eyed. A tear slid down her cheek, but she shook her head and moved to put Stryker between the Dom and herself. Her body barely touched Stryker's, but he could feel her trembling. He also knew she was shrugging into a shirt but didn't set down her belongings.

"Please get me out of here and I'll never ask you for anything ever again, Stryker. I'll stay out of your way and you'll never be bothered with me again. Just... please."

It was all Stryker could do not to growl. "Tobias. We're outta here."

"Got your six." It wasn't the first time Stryker was glad Tobias had his back. He led the way back through the club. He wanted to scoop Glitter up in his arms and hurry, but he needed his hands in case there was a fight. Besides, once she got her legs under her, she seemed to be good.

Somehow, before they'd made it through the club, Glitter had managed to get her pants on and only had her jacket in her hand. He caught her stuffing her underwear into the pocket before putting the jacket on.

"Bike's here." Stryker pointed, keeping his front to the door, while Tobias scanned the parking lot. "Get on."

She said nothing, but hurried to do what he commanded. He tossed her a helmet, and she put it on while he climbed in front of her and started his Hog.

"We get back to Angels, you and I gonna talk."

"Get me out of here and I'll do anything you want."

It was a loaded statement, especially after tonight. One she'd normally have said with a saucy grin and a wink. Now, Stryker knew she was dead serious.

The girl was a menace. To herself and everyone else. The best thing that could happen here was for her to listen to his lecture, promise never to go to the Dark again, then go home. Stryker knew it would be hard for him to allow that, though. He wanted to take her home with him. To the Salvation's Bane clubhouse where she'd be safe and guarded by all his brothers. But that wasn't happening. Not as long as she still worked at Salvation's Angels.

Well. That could change. And it just might if he didn't change his mind.

Chapter Three

The ride back to the club wasn't nearly long enough. What was she going to say to Stryker? Hell, what was she going to say to Thorn? It was his decree that the dancers at their strip clubs were not allowed to hang out at the clubhouse or to fraternize with the MC. Glitter racked her brain for something appropriately contrite, but came up empty. Her body hurt and her skin stung where Butcher had whipped her. It was what she thought she'd wanted, but she'd gotten more than she'd bargained for and had had no way to get out. She wanted to go home and soak in a hot bath. Her phone kept buzzing in her pocket and she just knew it was Butcher.

Butcher. Her "Dom." Well, he was for all of an hour. That was enough for Glitter. She knew he wouldn't let her go that easily, though she'd hoped. He'd singled her out the second she'd walked into the door. Said he'd seen her dance at Angels and had decided to make her his. Now she was in so much trouble she had no idea where to begin. Oh, she could absolutely confide in Stryker, but what was the point? He'd just yell at her. Sure, he'd take away the threat to his employee, but he'd hate her all the more for the extra effort he had to go through for her. Since she'd crushed on him from the moment she'd first laid eyes on him, that would be humiliating.

Tears burned her eyes. She almost never cried. Not only did she believe crying was useless, she was genuinely a happy person who always looked on the bright side of things. She kept the peace among the women at the club and just didn't let stuff get to her. This whole situation... had gotten to her.

The second Stryker stopped the bike in front of the converted firehouse on the outskirts of Palm Springs, Glitter hopped off and hurried inside. The club had converted it into a clubhouse, but several of the members lived there for various reasons. She had no idea where she was going, but she wasn't staying anywhere near Stryker. All the while, the phone in her pocket buzzed happily away. She still hadn't looked at it, so it could be one of her friends.

Yeah. Right.

As she looked around the common room, still moving at a steady clip toward the back of the room, she spotted Beast moving to intercept her.

"Glitter, you can't be here. You know that."

"Not my idea," she muttered, hiking a thumb over her shoulder, where she just knew Stryker followed. "Look. I need a place to shower and change clothes. Do you think Fleur could help me?"

Beast tilted his head at her as if what she said didn't compute. "You've been trying to get Stryker's attention forever. Looks like you got it. Why do you need Fleur?"

Glitter was about to her breaking point. "None of your Goddamned business!" She snapped the response before she could stop herself.

"OK, OK. Just calm down." Beast raised an eyebrow and put a hand on her shoulder, urging her toward the back of the room to the hallway.

"I am calm!" She really wasn't. Glitter was so emotional she was shaking. Not only was she scared out of her mind, but she was embarrassed and in pain as well. She took a deep breath, trying to calm herself but unable to slow the pounding of her heart. "Just... can I have a place to clean up?"

Beast kept hold of her shoulder and urged her out of the great room and into the hallway. He pulled out his phone and texted with his thumb before taking Glitter up the stairs. A few moments later, Fleur bounded down the stairs, a worried look on her face.

"Beast? What's wrong?"

Beast shrugged and gestured to Glitter. Fleur looked at Glitter, a bewildered but expectant look on her face. Fleur was a sweet woman. When Beast had found her at the Playground, she'd been beaten and almost raped. When the fuckers had been caught, none of them had fared well. If anyone would understand, it would be Fleur.

Glitter held Fleur's gaze as long as she could before giving a little sob and ducking her head, letting her long auburn hair cover her face.

"Oh, Glitter." Fleur lunged for her, wrapping her arms around Glitter. It was almost too much. Both the emotion and the physical pain of the lashes across her back nearly broke her.

"I just need a bath and clean clothes," she whispered to the other woman. "I have clothes, but I --"

"Shh, I know." Fleur wrapped her arm tightly around Glitter's waist and took her to a room a few doors down and urged her inside, shuttering the door behind them as they entered. "Are you hurt? Were you... assaulted?"

Glitter shook her head. "No." She wanted to say more, but couldn't bring herself to say she'd asked for it and then realized it was more than she could handle. When her phone buzzed again, she stiffened.

"That Stryker?" Fleur looked as if she fully expected Glitter to answer the phone, but there was no way in hell that was happening. Instead of answering, she just shrugged. "It doesn't matter." Fleur gave her a small smile. "Bathroom's over there. Soak in a hot bath. It will help. There's all kinds of toiletries. Me and the other ol' ladies try to keep the vacant rooms stocked just in case."

"Thanks," Glitter muttered.

When Fleur closed the door as she left, Fleur sagged against the wall of the bathroom before sliding down to sit in the corner in a heap. Her phone continued to buzz with both calls and text messages. Knowing she was going to have to obey the summons, Glitter unlocked her phone and pulled down the text menu. Dozens of texts. All from Butcher.

As she was scrolling through the increasingly threatening messages, she noticed several voice mails and shuddered to think what they said. Finally, she took a trembling breath and summed up the courage to listen to the last one.

"I told you if you ran from me you'd pay. You have until tomorrow night at eight to get your ass back to the Dark. You ain't there? I'll be comin' for you. Everything and everyone you ever loved, I'll destroy. They don't call me Butcher for no reason. You spill your guts to Salvation's Bane, I'll kill every single person ever associated with their club and their pathetic little sister club in Kentucky. You think that fucking hick state is far enough to get away from me? Think again, you little cunt. You've got a punishment coming, and it won't be easy. The longer you wait, the worse it will be."

The message ended. Glitter's hands went numb, and she dropped the phone on the floor. Maybe if she went back quickly, he'd make it easy on her. How had she gotten into this mess? It was supposed to be a one-time hook up at a BDSM club! This guy had no hold on her!

Except he did. As she scrolled through her texts, she saw pictures of her house. Inside her house. Her cat. Her dog. Her with friends from Angels and Bane. He'd basically documented her life. A killer fixated on her.

Glitter knew she should tell Thorn or Beast. As president and enforcer of Bane, both men would want to know. But if she told them and Butcher found out, or, worse, had her or the clubhouse bugged, Glitter had no doubt he'd at least try to make good on his promise. Though she'd only been with him a few hours, Glitter was convinced that, while Butcher might not be able to kill everyone, he was certainly capable of the attempt. She'd have to give this some thought.

A hot bath was just what she needed. Digging in the cabinet, she found some Epsom salts. Better than a bath bomb, to her mind. As she undressed, Glitter looked at the damage done to her back and torso in the mirror. Not horrible, but the evidence was still there. Thin welts were interspersed over her skin, given to her by Butcher wielding a thin whip. Even the memory made her break out in a sweat.

Sliding into the hot water was painful, and she couldn't stifle one small cry as she forced herself beneath the water to her neck. Maybe she should have pilfered the medicine cabinet for some painkillers before she started this venture.

It took several minutes, but gradually the stinging subsided and she started to feel better. When the water started to cool, she picked up some shower gel and lathered a washcloth. She was careful scrubbing her body, not wanting to hurt anything she'd just spent half an hour soothing. Knowing she was going to head back to the Dark, she didn't wash her hair. If she did, she'd have to dry it, and she just didn't have the energy for that.

What a fucking mess! She should have just told Thorn she wanted to go to the Playground as a guest. He probably wouldn't have let her, but at least she wouldn't be in the fix she was in currently.

As she dried and wrapped a towel around her, she noticed the welts on her body looked better. Still there, but not as angry. On the bed were some clothes Fleur had brought, including an unopened pack of underwear. Nothing fancy, but then, when did a stripper need fancy clothing? She snorted at her self-depreciation. This wasn't her. She made good money at Angels and made no apologies for it. For some reason, the whole experience with Butcher, the way he'd treated and talked to her, had been a real kick to her self-esteem and she really didn't know why.

Maybe because, once he had her consent to tie her up and gag her, he'd told her he'd been waiting to get his hands on her ever since he'd seen her at Salvation's Angels. He'd taken away her ability to use her safeword and her ability to get away from him, then he'd whipped her. There had been nothing sexual about it, which missed the entire point of why she was there in the first place. She needed the life she'd read about. At least, she needed it some of the time. A Dom who took care of her needs and wants and just took over when she was with him. Not all the time. Glitter had been on her own too long and was too independent for that. But she needed a safe place where she could just... be. She'd thought a Dom could do that for her. Maybe she'd just looked in the wrong place.

Whatever the problem, she was in deep now. Finding a way out was now her first priority. Dressed and her mind reset, Glitter took a deep breath before opening the door. Good thing, too, because standing outside her door, arms braced on the doorframe like he'd just been waiting for her to open the Goddamned door, was Stryker.

God! He was so… powerful looking! In jeans and a T-shirt that looked a couple sizes too small, his muscles rippled and bulged. His head of dark blond hair hung to his shoulders. His beard was full but short. Glitter couldn't remember ever seeing him smile. Not even with the girls at Salvation's Angels. He always seemed to have a frown on his face. Now it was even deeper. And he looked sexy as fuck.

She scowled at him. "What do you want?"

"That any way to talk to the man who rescued you from that place?"

"I know," she said with a little sigh. Glitter still couldn't meet his gaze. He'd seen her at her worst, and she was humiliated. "I'm sorry. But I need to go. Please."

"Where you goin'?" He didn't move an inch.

"Home." Good thing she wasn't looking him in the eye. Glitter thought she might have covered the wince but she wasn't sure.

"You can't lie worth a damn. You goin' back to that fuckin' club?"

Glitter put her shoulders back and made a valiant effort to meet his gaze. She skittered off before she could stop herself. "That's not your concern. I'm not supposed to be here. I needed to clean up and to think. I've done that. Now, I need to go."

Stryker still blocked her way. "Not good enough."

"Well, it's gonna have to be," she snapped. "Cause that's all you're getting."

"You want to go back? Back to that guy I rescued you from? 'Cause, I gotta tell ya, darlin', I thought you were smarter'n that."

"Don't belittle me, Stryker. I have a reason for what I'm doing. None of it's your business. I never said I was going back to him, but, if I am, it's none of your concern!"

"Think it is when I had to drag your ass out earlier. You're the one who wanted out." The reminder of that incident made her shiver. What would have happened if Stryker had left her there?

"Because I wasn't prepared. I am now."

Stryker finally dropped his arms from the doorframe, but he advanced on her, kicking the door shut as he stepped into her room, forcing her retreat. "You think so? You got any idea what a man like that does to women like you?"

"Women like me? What exactly does that mean?"

"Women like you. Innocent. Naive. You got no idea what's expected of you in a place like that. Why'd you let him gag you? You can't use a safeword if you can't talk, darlin'."

"I didn't know he was going to gag me. But, now that I know, I'll communicate in another way. Now. If you'll excuse me. I really need to leave. Thorn's generosity will only go so far."

"Ain't true, and we both know it. Thorn would never turn you out if you needed protection." Stryker looked at her then, tilting his head as if he were contemplating something. "That man threaten you?"

"No." Her answer was immediate.

"Uh huh." Stryker sighed, scrubbing a hand through his hair. "Fine. Go. Do what you have to. But don't believe that bullshit you spouted about Thorn not lettin' you stay here. You need us, you get your sweet ass over here. Got me?"

She nodded. For some reason, her eyes wanted to tear up. The reality was Stryker was a protective son of a bitch. She'd seen it many times at Angels when one of the girls got groped when she didn't want to be, or when a man simply wouldn't take no for an answer. Stryker had beat the shit out of more than one handsy man. But she wanted this time to be different. She wanted Stryker to actually care about her. In her heart, she knew this man could give her what she wanted, but she'd never ask him for it. She needed her job too much, and he was off limits. And this was the very reason why he was off limits. She was becoming possessive, and she had no right to be. With a force of will Glitter hadn't known she possessed, she fought back her tears. "I will. I really need to leave. Now."

Stryker didn't move out of her way. Instead, Glitter had to go around him to get to the door. She did so as quick as she could and hurried back to the main clubhouse. On the way, she requested an Uber. She wasn't relying on the club's generosity any more than she had to. Besides, she needed to get this over with. Her place right now was at the Dark. She'd go see what Butcher had in store for her, then get the fuck outta Dodge.

On the way out, several of the club members tried to make small talk with her, but Glitter brushed them off. It was uncharacteristic of her, but she just couldn't muster the energy to be sociable tonight. Thankfully, she didn't have to wait long for the Uber. Five minutes later, she was headed back across town. She texted Butcher and told him she was on her way. She had a feeling that, when the night was over, she'd wish she'd just gathered anything important to her and disappeared. She also had the feeling that, if she did, Butcher would make good on his promise to kill anything and anyone she loved.

Chapter Four

This was horseshit. Complete and utter horseshit. Stryker knew he was wrong to let Glitter leave the clubhouse. She might say she wanted to leave, but he knew she didn't. Could see it in her lovely face. Something was wrong, and he had to find out what.

First thing he had to do was get more information on Kiss of Death. He'd thought the club had imploded after their president had been killed. Apparently, they'd risen. Getting stronger if they were willing to encroach on a club like Bane's territory. With a club like Black Reign in the mix as well, it didn't bode well.

Bane had done more work than anyone to clean up the drug trade in Palm Beach. While there was no way to get rid of all of it, they'd slowed it down considerably. Neighborhoods once too dangerous for children to play in now flourished. They'd done their best not just to prevent the drugs from going to the streets, but help communities clean up their areas. The theory was that, if people were proud of their homes and neighborhoods, they'd care more about what went on. It also helped to have someone they could go to when they were too afraid to involve the police. Many of them found it easier to approach a biker than a cop. Especially when that biker had been working alongside them just the day before building a community center or a farmer's market or a playground. If this new club was owned by an MC like Kiss of Death, drugs were definitely involved.

"What the fuck's goin' on, man?" Havoc approached Stryker and Tobias as they leaned against the bar having a beer and hashing out what had happened at the Dark.

"Not sure. Might want to contact Justice. See if he's heard anything about a club from Nashville called Kiss of Death." As deflections went, this was a pretty good one.

"Ain't that the club that had Cain's ol' lady?"

"It is. We also believe they are the ones who've opened the Dark across town."

Havoc whistled. "Heard that place ain't what it seems. Women have disappeared from there. No one wants to report it because most have been daughters of wealthy citizens of Palm Beach. They don't want their family name soiled because their kid decided to slum it for the night. Probably figure the girls'll turn up sooner or later."

"Once anything is tied to that club, the fuzz'll be on the Playground like stink on shit." Tobias rubbed his chin. "We need to figure out what's going on and take care of it ourselves or be prepared to get rid of our business."

Stryker wasn't sure what he wanted to tell Havoc about Glitter. If he admitted his feelings for her, there'd be consequences. Besides, he had no idea how he really felt about her. He wanted her. But for how long? That was the fucking question. Thankfully, Tobias said nothing, just steered the conversation away from Glitter when Stryker knew that was what Havoc had come over to talk to them about.

There was a long silence while Stryker finished his beer. Tobias merely nursed his, keeping watch as always. Even among their brothers, they always made sure one of them was sober. It wasn't that they didn't trust the Salvation's Bane members, it was force of habit. They'd done the same thing as Green Berets. Besides, in their business dealings, one never knew when someone would try to ambush the club.

"So," Havoc said, raising his chin at the prospect working at the bar to signal he wanted a beer. "Wanna tell me what the fuck is goin' on with Glitter?"

So much for deflecting. Stryker shrugged. "Girl's exploring her sexuality, I guess. Thinks she needs a Dom."

Havoc stopped mid drink, lowering the bottle back to the bar and standing up straighter. "Dom. She's not going to the Playground. Beast would have said something."

"Nope." Stryker wasn't spelling it out for Havoc. Just thinking about how he'd found Glitter made his hackles rise.

"Fuck," Havoc said, scrubbing a hand over his face. "Only other BDSM club is two counties away. An hour or so." He paused. "She ain't goin'…"

Tobias took a sip of the coffee the prospect set in front of him. "Sure is. And that place needs to be burnt to the fuckin' ground."

"She gone willingly?"

"Far as I know." Stryker downed the rest of his beer. "Far as I fucking know."

"Why would she do that instead of just askin' for a night at the fucking Playground? Me and Beast woulda worked something out."

"You know how she is about rules." Stryker wanted to hit something but had no idea what. Correction. He wanted to take down that fuckin club. The Dark. Then he'd show Glitter what a true Dom was.

"If she's there on her own, there's not much we can do." Havoc watched Stryker closely. Stryker was very much afraid the man could see his emotions were plainly in evidence.

"There is. I just have to wait for the right time."

"Hope she doesn't get hurt in the process," Tobias said. "You need to go after her now."

"Can't do that, brother. You know I can't."

"Yeah, she'd probably never forgive you." Tobias paused. "Unless she actually needs you to take charge of her. Then who gives a fuck what she thinks. Get her out of danger. Worry about it later."

"Shut the fuck up, Tobias. I'll take care of her. I just need time to formulate a plan."

"Plan is get her the fuck out, then get her the fuck home."

"Not yet. She's not ready. At least she thinks she's not."

"How can you know? She looked pretty ready to me when we drug her out of that hell hole." Tobias was getting angry. With good reason, too. They all loved Glitter like a sister. Except him. Stryker just needed to know whether or not he was keeping her after this was over. He didn't want a permanent relationship. At least, he hadn't. Now...

"I'll take care of her. She just needs time to decide what she wants. I'm willing to give her that."

"Good," Havoc said. Turning to leave. "Just let us know what you need and when you need it, brother. 'Cause I have the feeling you're gonna need help with this one."

Stryker wasn't sure if he meant with Kiss of Death and the Dark... or with Glitter. Either would be possible.

* * *

Glitter stumbled from the Dark. Had it been a week since she'd first entered the club as a curious novice? It was all blurring together at this point. She was dressed, but knew blood seeped through her T-shirt in places. It was already full daylight as she wandered around the parking lot, trying to find her car but not really seeing anything around her. Who was she kidding? She wasn't in any shape to drive. But what else was she going to do? She had to get back home. No one was left at the club to help her. She didn't have a phone to call a ride. It was either drive or walk. Her car had been parked in the lot for twenty-four hours. Did she even have the keys?

Mind still in chaos, she kept walking. It was a slow drudge. Every step felt like shards of glass moving through her body. How was she still in one piece? How was she not a bloody mess of tattered flesh instead of only a few thin stripes leaking blood? Did it even matter? Apparently she felt worse than she looked because, though a few people gave her more than a passing glance, no one said anything to her or stopped her to see if she was OK. Or maybe no one wanted to get involved. Or cared.

It took her hours to finally make it to her house. The little house she'd rented from Salvation's Bane. She'd have to leave it soon. She couldn't stay. Not now. Not with what she'd been charged to do. It was Bane's life if she gave them up. Her life if she didn't. Glitter wasn't willing to give up the club that had taken her in, given her a place to live and a way to make money she could live with. Thorn had basically taken in a child and let her become an independent woman. No way could she repay that with betrayal.

She stumbled up the front steps only to realize she didn't have her keys. Now what was she going to do? She had to be at Salvation's Angels by three to get ready for the five o'clock open. She had no idea what time it was, but it had to be close to noon. Maybe after.

Somehow, she made it around the house to the back yard. She had a hammock strung between two palm trees. Climbing in with a prolonged whimper of pain, Glitter managed to drift off until the scorching sun woke her. If anything, she felt worse than before she'd slept. Again, she had no idea what time it was, but she knew she needed to get to the club. She had to work tonight. She'd missed four shifts this week without telling anyone where she was. If she didn't touch base soon, she wouldn't have a job. If she didn't have a job, she wouldn't have a home.

Briefly, she thought about calling Havoc. Or any of the girls. Just to let them know she still wanted to work there -- she just had some personal issues going on she couldn't talk about. Then she realized she had no idea where her phone was.

No. If she wanted a place to live, she had to get to work by any way possible. No money. No phone. No way to get into her house without breaking in. That meant she was walking. Thankfully, it wasn't too far. Maybe half an hour's walk. She could shower and change clothes at the club. No sweat.

Getting out of the damned hammock proved difficult and took more time that she would have thought. She'd lain there long enough for her body to become stiff and sore. The lashes covering her torso stung. Some because her shirt had stuck to them with dried blood and the friction of the shirt on the hammock tore the material free. In the end, though, she stood on her own.

One foot in front of the other. She just had to concentrate on that.

Time had no meaning for her. The sun was still high, but she couldn't focus on her surroundings enough to search out a digital clock on a billboard or anything. She might be extremely early, and no one would have the club open. She had her own key, but, again, had no idea where it was.

Thankfully, several of the girls were already there, and Glitter got inside without any trouble.

"Honey, you look like shit." Tanya looked at her, grinning widely. "Maybe you need a break. You know. Go to the clubhouse and get you a man for the night."

The other girls in the room stopped what they were doing. Likely, they'd all heard Stryker had taken her to the clubhouse. Some would resent her. Others would be curious. Most could give a fuck. Their money was made at Angels. They were like a club in themselves.

"Don't have the time or inclination to spar with you, Tanya." Glitter pushed past the other woman and headed to the bathroom. Before she could make it, however, the other woman continued her taunting.

"Missed you this week. Seems you got better shit to do. Bigger fish to fry, huh? Might wanna get on that, little Miss Thang. If not..." She let the implication drag on. Glitter stopped, not wanting to turn around to face the other woman, but her body betrayed her by doing it anyway. "Yeah. I bet you'll take a trip to the butcher if you don't."

She knew. Somehow, Tanya knew. That meant that Butcher had people on the inside. Probably more than just Tanya. Oh, God! If even a stripper paid by Kiss of Death had gotten inside one of Bane's clubs, didn't that mean that the person on the inside had to be someone high up in the inner workings of club? And was it really Salvation's Bane or just someone they employed at Salvation's Angels?

She wasn't smart enough -- or brave enough -- to do this by herself. Glitter tried to give the other woman a scathing retort, but the blood had drained from her face, and it was all she could do to stand. Finally she settled on, "Mind your own business, you little crack whore." It was all the threat she could muster. If Havoc or Thorn found out she was selling at the club, the consequences for Tanya would be far more severe than anything Butcher would dish out to Glitter. And that was saying a great deal. Bane did not tolerate anyone betraying them. Dealing inside the club was the biggest betrayal outside of spying on them. Glitter had no idea if it worked or not, but Tanya didn't follow her into the locker room. Thank goodness too. Glitter didn't want anyone to see her in this state. She knew she looked like hell. Taking her clothes off was only going to reveal more ugliness.

With a grimace, she jumped into the shower, trying her best to scrub the welts and shallow cuts with soap. It wasn't nearly enough to disinfect, but maybe it was better than nothing. It stung horribly in places, but Glitter was too focused on her problems to really notice.

Out of the shower, she dressed hurriedly. She'd chosen a gauzy little number for tonight. Didn't really go with the music, but it was easier on and off, and she wasn't sure she could keep from screaming if she had to wear anything tight to her skin.

"Glitter?"

Was that Havoc? Oh, God! Why was he invading the women's shower? He never did that.

"Glitter? You in there?"

"Yes. Don't come in! I'll be right out."

"Just come to my office when you're done. Don't be long."

She froze. Was this a test? Was Havoc the man inside? He was the vice president of Bane. Most of the men had been together for years. Would Havoc betray them all with another club? One so vile and vicious? She didn't think so. Couldn't see it no matter how hard she looked. But was she willing to risk her life? The lives of the people she cared about most? Stryker wouldn't see it coming. He trusted his brothers. So, if Havoc betrayed them, Stryker would have an accident, and no one would know. Except her.

Glitter took a shuddering breath and slumped in defeat. She wouldn't give up the club. Not that she could tell Butcher anything anyway. But she wouldn't warn them either. Stryker would just go to Havoc or Thorn, and she couldn't risk it. She'd just have to figure this out on her own.

With a heavy heart and a broken spirit, Glitter trudged to Havoc's office. She was dressed for her set onstage, but she'd never felt less sexy in her life. She was at least clean from the Dark, but she didn't look her best. Oh, well. Maybe the shadows would be enough to cover most of the damage when she was on stage. Maybe.

Outside Havoc's office, Glitter knocked softly twice. When he didn't answer immediately, she turned to go. She could pretend she thought he wasn't there. Unfortunately, the door opened, and he stood there, larger than life and twice as scary. Thinking he might be the plant inside Salvation's Bane gave him a sinister quality she'd never noticed before. Glitter glanced at him once briefly before looking back down at the floor.

"Come inside, Glitter." He didn't sound unkind or threatening. He sounded almost... concerned? "Have a seat."

"I really need to get to the stage. It's nearly time for me to go on."

"I know, but we need to have a quick talk."

"What about?"

He was silent for so long, Glitter lifted her eyes to him just to make sure he was still in the conversation. She found him staring at her intently.

"Wanna tell me what's goin' on?"

"Nothing," she said softly.

"Really? You've missed several shifts this week. No call, no show. Most girls'd be gone after the second one. You've been workin' here for two years. Worked at Beach Fit for almost four years before that. Never in any of that time have you missed even a single day. Call in or not. Definitely didn't just no show. You're also the best employee we've ever had either place. That's the only reason I'm not firing you." He crossed his arms over his chest, looking stern and more than a little miffed. She definitely owed him an explanation, but what to say? "Try again, Glitter."

"It- it's personal," she finally settled on. "I'll get my shit worked out. It won't touch work again, Havoc."

Again, there was a long silence before Havoc spoke. "Not good enough." Glitter's world plummeted. What was she going to do? "I'll let it go for now. But you're gonna tell someone what's happening, and we're going to help you fix it." She looked up sharply, but he continued. "Because you're family, Glitter. That's what family does." He reached for her hand and she took it. He pulled her gently to her feet. "Get ready for your set. You probably don't have long."

Glitter was so upset she was shaking. How was she going to get through this? She caught a glimpse of herself in one of the mirrors inside the dressing room as she breezed through. There were dark circles under her eyes no amount of concealer was going to hide.

Her hair was limp and lackluster. The outfit she had on didn't fit, hanging on her more than it should, making her look more like a shapeless blob of pastel than an exotic dancer. Oh well. There was nothing for it now. She could hear them announcing her even now.

As she hurried to the stage wing entrance, several of the girls called out to her. Glitter ignored them. She had to focus on getting out there and doing her job, or there was no way she made it through the next five minutes. Just five minutes. Less, even. If she could do that, she'd have more time to straighten herself up before the next number. Just five minutes. She could do this.

The second she appeared in the spotlight, the crowd cheered and clapped, expecting the show she always gave them. Glitter loved her job. Loved dancing. Even baring her body was a thrill. It wasn't purely sexual, as much as her little contribution to humanity. If men liked looking at her, if it made someone happy, why not give it to them? They weren't touching her that much, and she had regulars who she knew had unhappy home lives -- from spouses they should never have married for whatever reason, to sick loved ones, to high-pressure jobs they couldn't escape -- who always tipped her well and were never inappropriate with her. Some came to the club specifically to see her. She'd been dancing there for two years. It was natural she'd pick up some fans.

Time to get to work. For them. She could do this for the people in the audience counting on her to make their day a little bit better. She gave them her signature smile as she twirled, letting the gauzy material swirl around her freely, giving glimpse of her bare body beneath.

She'd just started to peel off one scarf when she caught sight of someone at the end of the stage. At first, the only thing that caught her attention was how big he was. Even in a stripper club owned by bikers, the man stood out. He sat at the bar surrounding the runway where the girls danced and teased, just close enough for the men to tuck their tips into the garters around the girl's thighs, but not so close he could actually get to her easily or too quickly for the bouncer to intervene, should the inclination arise. As he took a sip of his whisky, the lights around the stage swung in the programmed arc and one briefly illuminated his face.

Butcher.

Reflexively, Glitter stumbled backwards, hand clutching her throat. She didn't have on his collar. She'd taken it off in the shower. He'd warned her before she left the Dark that, if she took it off, he'd be "extremely displeased." For a short time, she stood frozen, staring at him, unable to even breathe.

"Glitter?" One of the older men near her at the front of the stage reached up to tuck a bill into her garter. He was a regular, coming in at least three times a week since Glitter had started at Salvation's Angels. When she looked at him, she saw worry on his face. He glanced from her to the big man at the opposite end of the stage. "You OK?"

She nodded, then tried to snap out of it, continuing with her dance. She gave him a smile, though she imagined it looked a little maniacal. "I'm good, Charlie. Just stumbled a little. Thanks for worrying."

"Can't have my girl in distress." He smiled back, but she could tell he wasn't buying it.

Glitter continued to shed scarves one at a time. Halfway through the song, she had everything off but the one surrounding her torso. The second she whipped it off, in her usual dramatic fashion, the noise of the crowd died down. Some still whooped and hollered, but most of the din subsided until only the music remained.

Glancing around her, she saw several of the men with grim faces. Charlie looked horrified. No one moved for several long seconds. Fear seized her and Glitter's gaze went straight to Butcher. He had a knowing smirk on his face, his arms crossed over that massive chest.

At a loss, she started to dance again. She really had no idea what was wrong with everyone. But when Charlie crawled up on the bar and up to the stage, dragging his coat with him, Glitter stopped once again.

"Who did this, sweet girl? Tell me, and I'll make sure one of your biker men know. Bastard needs to die." He spoke as he draped his coat around her shoulders, pulling her to him to shield her front.

A sharp whistle pierced the hard pounding of the music and an instant later, Charlie passed her off to someone else. She found herself being lifted and moved off the stage. Gradually the noise faded away, but Glitter had no idea where she was. She looked up to see who had carried her away, only to find Stryker's grim face looking straight ahead. He looked pissed. Probably because she'd ruined the mood in the bar. What had she done? Why had Charlie jumped on the runway and covered her?

Tired. She was so fucking tired.

She must have dozed off, because the next thing she knew she was being lifted out of a vehicle. Something high up, because when Stryker lifted her into his arms, she knew there was a downward motion. She whimpered, stiffening. "Where are we?"

"Shh. Just relax. You're OK."

"No, I'm not! He'll find me." She was trembling now, scared to her core. Glitter tried to get out of Stryker's arms, but he was so much stronger than her.

"Don't," he growled. "You don't get to fight me now."

Tears were coming. She knew they were. There was nothing she could do to stop them, either. Burying her face in Stryker's chest, she just let them come. Thankfully, it wasn't a body-wracking cry. Tears just silently leaked from her eyes, but there was no stopping them.

Glitter wasn't fully aware of what was going on, but sooner than she'd have liked, Stryker put her down. He was putting her on a bed, but she hadn't heard anyone else around them. If they were in the clubhouse, no one else was there.

"Wh-where are we?" She was hesitant to ask, but had to know how many people had witnessed this particular walk of shame.

"My home," was his gruff reply. He urged her to lie on her front. When she put her head on her arms, he turned her head so that she was facing away from him.

"What are you doing?"

"Giving you privacy, since you won't have any for a while."

She figured she should question him on that, but just didn't have the energy. Besides, it was just easier to follow his instructions. Let him have control for a while. Later, she might put up a fight. When he tried to make her tell him what was going on. But now, she'd just relax and do what he told her.

Chapter Five

The thing that bothered Stryker most about this whole fucking situation was that he hadn't noticed the state Glitter was in. What had brought him to the stage in the first place had been seeing another man -- even if he was in his sixties -- pulling her in for a hug. At least, that was what he'd thought for the first second. Then he'd realized how quiet the place had gone underneath the music. Once he'd pushed his way to the stage and taken her from the old guy, Charlie had looked him in the eyes and said, "If you did that to this sweet girl, I'll fuckin' kill you."

Stryker believed him.

When Stryker had turned her around, he'd seen the numerous cuts and welts all over her front. He assumed her back had been the same. As she lay on the bed before him, he found his assumption was dead on. Glitter was covered in the things. Even her arms and legs, though to a lesser degree. How the fuck had he not noticed? He knew Havoc had talked to her about missing work. How had the other man not noticed? Fuck!

He tried to give himself time to process. To just take in the marks all over her and accept it had happened. He could deal with whoever had done it later. Right now had to be about Glitter. He had to find something inside him gentle enough to take care of her.

The time it took to get peroxide, some cotton balls, and the antibiotic cream wasn't nearly enough. After texting Blade that his assistance was needed, he went back into the bedroom adjoining his bathroom. Glitter still lay as he'd left her, shivering slightly.

"Should have covered you," he muttered and picked up a fleece blanket he had draped across a chair. He never used it, but when one of the ol' ladies had decorated his house, she'd put the thing there in case he met someone who liked to sit by the window. Apparently, she'd thought a fuzzy blanket had been needed. Why was beyond him. In Florida, it wasn't typically necessary. Now, he had to remember to find out who had left it and thank her.

"Thank you," she murmured. Her voice was quiet. Defeated sounding. It broke Stryker's heart and made him want to go on a killing rampage.

Just so she realized her reprieve wasn't going to be a long one, he told her what was getting ready to happen. "I've called in the club doc. His name's Blade. Did a stint in Pararescue and is a damned good surgeon. He has a private practice here in Palm Springs, but he's also a member of Salvation's Bane. I say that because I want you to know you can trust him. Besides. I wouldn't let anyone near you I thought might hurt you in any way. Get me?"

"Yeah," she said.

She still didn't look at him, which surprised Stryker. "Can you turn your head to look at me, honey?" For a moment, Stryker thought she wasn't going to move. Then she carefully turned her head so she faced him.

"Thank you." He pulled a chair close to the bed and sat so that when he rested his elbows on his knees, he was closer to eye level with her. "Once Blade's examined you, me and you are gonna have a little talk."

She whimpered, but when he said nothing else, she nodded her head slightly.

"Good. No lies, Glitter. I don't tolerate them on the best of days, and this isn't one. You will tell me the truth. Every single detail. In return, I promise not to freak out and go on a killin' spree. At least, not today."

Again, she nodded, though she closed her eyes as one tear leaked from the corner of her eye across the bridge of her nose to the pillowcase.

"Good. Blade will be here in about ten minutes. Until then, I want you to rest. Once he's here, we have to clean you up and dress those cuts. You will do exactly as we tell you."

Again, she nodded.

"Gonna need the words this time, babe. I have to know you understand I would never let him in here if I thought he'd hurt you on purpose. Because I imagine that when we get to cleaning some of these wounds, it's gonna hurt."

"I understand," she said softly. Stryker sat back in the chair, but she spoke again. "He'll come for me, Stryker. He'll never let me go."

"Who, honey?"

"Butcher," she whispered. "I wasn't supposed to take off his collar, but I did. He was in the club tonight."

Stryker froze. "In the club. Angels?"

"Yes. And Tanya. She's working for the new MC in town selling drugs. If she and Butcher got in, there's someone else letting them in."

"That why you didn't tell Havoc what was goin' on tonight when he talked to you? You think he's rattin' out his club?"

She shrugged, then winced. "I don't know. Seems ridiculous now, but how else did they get in the club?"

"I can see your dilemma." He held her gaze for long moments, needing her to look into his eyes and know he was taking her seriously. "I will thoroughly check into this before I speak to anyone. Including Havoc. But I can tell you now that you have nothing to worry about from Bane. Tanya doesn't matter. Butcher does."

She shook her head. "It was stupid. I'm sure I wasn't thinking clearly."

"Doesn't matter. You make a valid point. I'll go over everything before I mention this to anyone. If there is someone on the inside helping them out, I'll know who and why before anyone else is brought in." He reached out and took one of her hands, gripping it firmly. "I will protect you from anyone, Glitter. Anyone. You get me?"

It took a long, long while. Glitter's eyes never left his. She seemed to be deciding whether or not to believe him. Stryker was patient. The main thing he'd learned during his time in the Marine Force Recon was patience. He was also very good at finding people who didn't want to be found. That wasn't to say he believed for even a hot second Havoc had betrayed the club. He didn't. But he would keep his word to Glitter because he did trust Havoc and every other member of Salvation's Bane. Which was why, once Blade had checked her out and she'd had a night's sleep, he was taking her back to the clubhouse and shutting that place down until he got to the bottom of this.

Blade entered the room without announcing his presence in the house. Typical of the bastard. He'd been Pararescue, but he was quiet as any Force Recon. Glitter gasped, but didn't move, her gaze searching out his for reassurance.

"It's OK. It's just Blade. Remember?"

"Coulda knocked," she grumbled.

"Yeah, that's not his style."

Blade set an old-fashioned medical bag on the bed and sighed down at her. "Got herself into trouble?"

Stryker shrugged. "Something like that, maybe. But not by choice."

Blade's eyes snapped to Stryker's. Stryker held his gaze for long moments. Then Blade carefully peeled away the blanket revealing Glitter's back. He dropped the blanket back in place like it had burned him, still making no noise.

"You get the bastard?"

"Not yet."

"I'll go with you when you take him down."

Glitter whimpered. Stryker took her hand and brought it to his lips before he thought better of it. She needed reassurance. He could give that to her. "You have to know we're not letting this bastard get away with hurting you like this," he said gently.

"But... just not tonight. Right?"

"No, baby. Not tonight."

* * *

The only thing that got her through letting another man see her this way was Stryker's hand firmly holding hers through the whole thing. The talk they were getting ready to have wasn't going to be a pleasant one. She knew that. One of two things was getting ready to happen. Either Stryker lost his shit and went to kill Butcher tonight, or, worse, he did nothing. Glitter thought she'd shatter if he blew this off. Not going to kill Butcher meant he didn't care about her. Not like she cared about him. Stryker defended those he loved to the death. His club. His brothers. Even if he did go after Butcher and Kiss of Death, how would she know he was going because of her or because they were a danger to Salvation's Bane?

"Feel better?" Stryker sat next to the bed where she'd been lying on her side. He and Blade had put her in one of Stryker's shirts because it basically swallowed her and wouldn't stick to or abrade her skin. Before he'd left, Blade had given her a shot of antibiotics and a pain pill. He'd tossed the bottle in Stryker's general direction and muttered some instructions, but Glitter didn't pay attention. Stryker left her alone for the better part of an hour, during which she'd dozed lightly.

"Yeah," she said. "A few places sting, but not badly. My ass hurts where he gave me that stupid shot." She tried to lighten the mood, but Stryker just gave her a slow nod. His facial expression didn't change.

"I imagine it does." Silence again. Then he sat back in the chair.

Defeated, Glitter sighed and tried to sit. Stryker placed a gentle hand on her shoulder, shaking his head.

"I knew I couldn't go to the Playground. Not and work at Salvation's Angels."

"But you do go to Fetish Factory in Miami."

She gasped. "How did you know that?"

"I keep tabs on my employees."

"So you knew about Tanya."

"I did. My suspicion is that she was responsible for getting Butcher inside, but I will find hard proof before I go to anyone, because I told you I would."

"I'm such an idiot." She sniffed. "I should have realized you'd know everything going on around there."

"It's my job, honey."

That stung. But of course she was just a job to him. She was a stripper in a club owned by his MC. They had rules for a reason. If he treated her like anything other than valuable property, it would become too personal. From what she'd witnessed of the guys in Bane, they were all possessive and alpha to a fault. No way they let a woman they considered theirs dance in a club. Even their own.

"You're wrong, you know," he said, sliding a little off course, but Glitter was grateful. She really didn't want to talk about this.

"About what?"

"You're not just a job to me." He raised a hand to stop her when she opened her mouth. "And before you deny that's what you were thinking, you're transparent as fuck. Can always tell what you're thinking by the look on your face."

"If I'm not a job to you, then…"

"Then what are you?" When she nodded, Stryker sighed. "You're gonna be my woman. You ain't yet, which is the only reason Tanya gets to live if she let Butcher in. I never claimed you in front of the club or the girls at the club. That changed with the first phone call I made after I carried you off stage. I'll make it official the second I'm able. And to your next question, no. I'd prefer you not dance anymore, but I'm also not a dick." He paused, then shook his head slightly. "OK, sometimes I'm a dick. But that's not the point. As long as no one touches, and as long as I'm with you, I have no problem with men seeing what they'll never have. You make sure you save your private dancing for me, and I'll have no problem with you continuing to dance. If that's what you want."

"That's surprising," she said, blinking up at him.

He shrugged. "Lucy, Vicious's woman, dances. Hell, she sometimes dances at parties we have. She's with Vicious and everyone knows it. He doesn't mind showin' her off. Don't mind fuckin' her either. Sometimes they make it to a private place. Other times not. Yeah, we're a bit possessive, but as long as there are boundaries we all set and enforce, I got no problem with you doin' something you love."

"I do love dancing, but maybe I could just, I don't know. Dance for you." Glitter felt shy saying it. What if he rejected her, no matter what he'd just said?

"I think I'd like that best of all. Now. I diverted you. Continue."

Strangely, the direction of their conversation had given her courage. "You truly mean what you said? You want me to be your woman? Does that mean you want me as your ol' lady?"

"Absolutely," he said without hesitation. "It's gonna happen. Might have to be with you kickin' and screamin' but it's gonna happen."

A shiver ran through her at the look he gave her. If she had any doubts before, that look erased them. This man was deadly serious.

"OK," she said, clearing her throat. "So, I needed to go to a club, but didn't want to drive to Miami. I suppose I could have gone to the one in West Palm Beach, but they only allow nonmembers on certain nights."

"I take it the Dark isn't so picky?"

She shook her head, looking down at her hands. "About anything. The contracts they have are full of workarounds and double talk. Sure, I got a safe word, but the first thing he did was gag me. Because I didn't say I was opposed to being gagged in the contract. It wasn't on the check boxes, and I didn't think to write it in." When she paused, Stryker urged her on. "Butcher picked me out the second I walked in the door. Someone snagged me and brought me to him. The night you found me was the first time I'd been there. He didn't tell me why he wanted me, only that if I didn't come back, he'd kill everyone I've ever loved." She looked at her hands. "Since my family's dead and I've been on my own since I was fourteen, the only people I had to worry about were the girls at Angels. And Bane. I figured out later he'd been watching the women at Angels, just waiting to find someone who could be a spy. Tanya was an easy recruit, but she hasn't been there long, and she doesn't know anything."

"But when he saw you, he figured he had the perfect in."

"Only I don't know anything either. I went back that night because he'd threatened Salvation's Bane. I wouldn't have given him anything even if I knew anything to tell him, but not going meant an attack on the club, and I didn't know who I could trust."

"You can trust me, Glitter. You should have come to me."

"And have you played straight into his hands if one of the guys had been a rat? I wasn't thinking rationally so I didn't see how stupid that sounded then, but I wouldn't have risked it even if I had. Angels and Bane are the only family I have left." Tears started again, and Glitter knew it would be a long, long time before she had enough control to stop them. "I would do anything to protect my family!"

Stryker moved then, sitting on the bed and pulling her into his lap. Strong arms crushed her to a broad, muscled chest and held her head to him while she sobbed. "I've got you, baby. No one is going to hurt you again. Not ever." He kissed the top of her head, stroking damp hair away from her face. "One more thing and I won't ask you questions any more tonight. Can you tell me why you went to those BDSM clubs to begin with? Do you live that lifestyle?"

"N-no. I-I was just c-curious," she managed to get out. "I-I'd read th-that in a D/s relationship, the s-sub could j-just let g-go when th-things got to b-be too much."

"Ah, I see. You were orphaned at fourteen. Been living on your own since. I imagine running from the system until you turned eighteen?"

"Y-yeah. I-I didn't w-want another family. My b-best friend in s-school was a f-foster. I s-saw the bruises on h-her. Decided I c-could take care of m-myself." The tears just kept coming. It seemed like the longer they talked, the more everything just had to get out.

"You did, too. I know you started working at Beach Fit when you were fourteen. You must have nearly run straight to us."

"I had to fuck a guy to get my fake ID in order to get a job outside of prostitution. Sick, huh? I decided then I was never gonna prostitute myself again. For any reason. I didn't mind stripping. I had all the power," she said, sniffing. "I got to say who and what. At least, that's the way it was at Angels. I snuck in and just listened to them. Then went to Havoc for a job."

Stryker snorted. "I remember that. He called you out, then practically dragged you down to Beach Fit and put you to work."

A fresh flood of tears spilled from her eyes. "He even put me in a house! Bane has been so good to me. You. Havoc. Everyone. Don't you see I couldn't let any of you get hurt because of me?" The sobs came then, and wouldn't stop.

"I know, honey. I know. It's all right. Everything's gonna be fine now. I've got you. Ain't never lettin' you go."

"St-Stryker?"

"Yeah, baby."

She sniffed and looked up at him. God, he was rugged! Tats creeping up his neck behind his ear. That stern expression that looked like he never smiled and was ready to take on death if necessary. She thought he could win against anyone and anything coming his way. He was strong. Capable. And had a heart no one saw through the exterior. "I love you. I have since the day I met you. I know you don't love me back, and that's OK, but --"

He put his hand over her mouth. "Shut the fuck up," he growled. "Don't presume to know how I feel. I said I'm takin' you as my woman, didn't I?" He didn't move his hand, so she just nodded. "Don't do no good claimin' a woman I don't love. Just makes everyone miserable. This way, at least I won't be miserable. I got what I want. Gives me the incentive I need to make you happy. If you already love me, it'll make that part easier." He removed his hand only to cover her mouth with his.

The kiss was gentle, coaxing even, but the power he wielded over her was obvious. He was a dominant lover, one who could give her what she needed. With one sweep of his tongue, the gentleness faded, and he became demanding, almost rough in taking the kiss he wanted. Then he pulled back, looking straight into her eyes. "Now. Tell me. What is it you want? What do you hope to gain from goin' to clubs like that?"

This was it. This was when she rolled over and showed her belly. Her weakness. "I've been on my own since I was fourteen. I just want someone to take care of me every now and then. Sometimes, I get overwhelmed. If anything goes wrong in my life, I have to 'adult.' Sometimes, I just don't want to. I can't. I know that makes me weak, and I accept that. But I just don't want to have to do it all the time. When it gets to be too much…"

"You want to have someone who takes over until you can recuperate."

"Yes." Glitter ducked her head. "It doesn't happen often, but this is one of those situations. I was hoping to eventually meet someone who could be that for me. It didn't even have to be a lover. Just a friend. Someone who could help me when I needed them."

"OK." Stryker pulled her head back to his chest, stroking her hair again. "I think it's time for bed. Why don't you go wash your face? Can you make it on your own?"

"Yeah," she said with a sigh. She really didn't want to get up. She loved Stryker. Like a woman loves a man. With her whole heart and body. She'd give him anything he wanted. Do anything to satisfy his needs, in or out of bed. But Stryker was thirty-nine years old. He likely saw her as a kid he needed to protect. Sadly, this week, she'd proven to be exactly that.

When she returned from the bathroom, he had the bed turned down and stood next to it in his boxer briefs and nothing else. His cock was hard to miss, stretching with interest as she walked into the room. Glitter averted her face, not so much embarrassed but uncomfortable because she didn't know what was expected of her. For her part, she wanted to sink to her knees and worship that part of him until she drove him out of his mind with wanting her.

"Get in," he ordered gruffly. When she did, he crowded in next to her, pulling her into his arms and tightly against his body. His cock pressed insistently into the crease of her ass, seeking refuge. "Now. Sleep."

"You've got to be kidding." Glitter barked out a laugh, looking over her shoulder at him. "I can't sleep like this!"

He squeezed her to him even harder. "Like how? In my arms? Or with my cock nestled in the crack of your ass?"

"Either!" She squeaked. "You can't expect me to lie here, knowing you want more -- and if that aforementioned cock in the crack of my ass doesn't mean you want me then you're a pink unicorn -- and wanting more myself. God!"

"You can just call me Stryker."

"Ohh! You're impossible."

He chuckled as he brushed his lips over her neck. "No. And if you were in any shape for this, I'd be fucking you into the morning. You ain't. Don't mean I'm givin' up an opportunity to hold you close to me. Tomorrow or the next day. You're gonna be better. Then I'm not lettin' you leave my side -- or my bed -- for a long, long while. When that happens, when you're mine, you turn everything over to me. I'm in charge. That means you don't worry about anything other than what I tell you. I promise, that will only be pleasing me. Easy enough, yeah?"

"Oh. Well." She cleared her throat. "When you put it like that."

Stryker continued to nuzzle her neck, placing light kisses up and down her skin. It wasn't long before her eyelids drooped and she simply shut them.

Chapter Six

Being manager of Salvation's Angels had its perks. One of which was access to the remote camera feeds. Not just the official ones either. There were numerous hidden ones throughout the facility only he had access to. Basically, there was not a nook or cranny off limits. Even the bathrooms. He supposed a voyeur could have a field day, but that wasn't the reason he'd set up these cameras. It was for times like these.

He followed Tanya's movements throughout the club over the last month. Only one person seemed to be working with her, and it was exactly who Stryker had suspected. Another dancer who came on about the same time Tanya did. Both women were selling drugs in the club, and both had been seen in or around the Dark. Which meant they likely knew this Butcher. A round of phone calls to his usual sources, then one to a more unusual but necessary and highly effective source. Justice might be in a maximum-security prison, but he knew the goings on in Palm Beach as well anyone roaming the streets on a daily basis.

"Your girl's in a heap a trouble," Justice's gruff, rumbly voice told him over the phone. "Butcher not only wants information he thinks she has, but he's taken a fancy to her. Keep her away from him unless you don't care if he has her."

"She's my woman, Justice. I plan on killin' that fucker."

"I see. What do you need from me?"

"She's afraid there might be someone else involved. Trying to wave it off now that she's told me everything. Says she trusts me, but I promised her I'd make damned sure before I went to Thorn."

"She's afraid one of the brothers sold her out."

"In a nutshell, yeah. It's why she hasn't already told Havoc, or at least that's what she says. I think she wanted to tell me, but I was an asshole." He muttered that last bit, not wanting to admit to handling her wrong, but not wanting Justice to think badly of Glitter.

"Understood. Give me twenty-four hours. I'll be in touch."

* * *

It was almost noon when he went to wake Glitter. She hadn't moved since he'd left her bed. He'd hated leaving her at all, but he had had to put things in motion, because he wasn't letting this Butcher fucker live one second longer than strictly necessary. He sat on the edge of the bed and sifted his fingers through her hair. "Wake up, baby."

She moaned and stretched, the sound shooting straight to his cock. "What time is it?" God, that voice! Was there anything about her he didn't find sexy?

"Noon. You seemed like you could use the rest, so I let you sleep."

Glitter yawned before rubbing her eyes. When she'd had time to get her bearings, she met his gaze. Her face was void of emotion, but he could see the vulnerability in her eyes. "Did you go after him?"

"Told you I wouldn't until I'd looked into it thoroughly. Also promised I wouldn't go on a killing spree the same day you told me."

"I guess it was after midnight when you promised that." She gave him a small grin.

"Don't worry, though. Got a reevaluation in about sixteen or so hours. Once I can confirm exactly who was involved with letting Butcher into the club, and on what level, I'll get down to business."

"You told Thorn?"

"Now you're pissin' me off," he growled. "Told you I'd thoroughly investigate this shit before I went to anyone else inside the club. I'm using a brother who's currently not in the area. He's in prison, but he knows more about what's goin' on with the clubs in the area than we do. Always has. Seems like he knows even more now. He says they're all clean, then I go to Thorn and Havoc. Until then?" He spread his arms. "It's just you and me, kid."

She frowned. "I've not been a kid in a long time, Stryker. Not since I was fourteen."

"I know. Which is why I can take you as my woman and still have some self-respect." He held out a hand to her. "Come on. Let's eat."

She shook her head, pushing off the covers and pulling her shirt over her head. "Not yet."

Stryker drank in her naked body like a starving man at an all-you-can-eat buffet. "Fuck," he muttered. "Where to fucking start?"

"Wherever you want to, Stryker."

He scrubbed a hand over his mouth, then over the back of his neck. "If we do this, Glitter, ain't no goin' back. I knew I wanted you before you danced for me. Now, I know, once I have you, you ain't gettin' away from me. I'll protect you with my life, but you'll be mine to do with as I please."

"Can I tell you something without you judging?"

The uncertain look on her face made Stryker want to punch something. He'd always thought of Glitter as a strong, confident woman. Even at fourteen, she'd been so full of life and determined to make a life for herself he'd never really thought there could be a vulnerable side to her.

"I'll never judge you for telling me what you think, Glitter. Never. Now, say what's on your mind."

"I've only had sex a few times. Once when I was fourteen to get my fake ID. After that, I swore it would only be with someone I wanted. Someone I chose. Since then, I've had one lover, and he didn't last long."

"He hurt you?"

"No. He just wasn't as interested in me as I was in him. And that's OK. But, Stryker, I couldn't stand it if you left me after this. So, you're telling me you're not letting me go once you fuck me. I'm holding on to that with both hands. Not only holding you to it, but promising you that I'll go to the ol' ladies if you decide to try and leave me. I might need to be submissive sometimes, to let you take control, but I'm not shy about hanging on to what I want."

Something inside Stryker's chest relaxed. He hadn't even been aware he was tense, but hearing her confession was like a balm to his every wound.

"You got nothing to worry about, baby. It's you for me. Always has been."

"Then make love to me. I might be a little sore, but it's all superficial. If you'll just take me to a world of sensation and pleasure, nothing else will matter."

"You promise to tell me if something hurts?"

"I promise."

"Good." Then he kissed her.

* * *

Hurt? How could anything he did to her possibly hurt? Glitter clung to Stryker as he swept his tongue inside her mouth and claimed all her kisses for the rest of her life. Being in his strong arms was everything she'd dreamt it would be.

Stryker maneuvered her so he lay between her legs, pressing his cock against her sex. He was still fully clothed, and she was naked as the day she was born. His hands slid around her back and he rolled over slowly, bringing her with him. His slid his hands up to grip her ass possessively. Glitter couldn't help her moan, especially when he squeezed both cheeks, kneading gently.

"Yes," she gasped when he slid his lips across her cheek and to her neck. "Oh, God!"

"Ain't no saint, Glitter. And the things I'm gettin' ready to do to you are beyond wicked. You ready?"

"So ready. So fucking ready."

Stryker sat up, his arms once again wrapping around her tightly. She let her head fall back, giving him access to her breasts. Greedily, he pulled one tip into his mouth, sucking strongly before moving to the other. He growled around the nipple and slid his hands back to her ass, continuing to knead her tender flesh.

Glitter was desperate to get him naked. She needed this more than she'd ever needed anything in her life. Clawing at his shirt, she pulled it over his head as he chuckled at her impatience.

"Greedy little girl. Do you want me naked?"

"I do! Need you inside me, Stryker."

Once his shirt was off, Glitter rubbed herself shamelessly over his naked skin. She released a long moan at the pleasure just pressing herself against his warm body caused. God, she loved this man! He shuddered beneath her touch as much as she did with his. His cock pressed against her naked cunt through his jeans, making him groan when it throbbed.

"Gonna be the death of me, woman."

"Me? What about you? You still have too many clothes on!"

He chuckled and laid her down on the bed before standing. She raised herself up on her elbows to watch as he shed his jeans and underwear. His cock sprang free, bobbing proudly in front of her. He grabbed it and pumped it lazily, never taking his eyes off her.

"Holdin' you to your word, Glitter. You ain't leavin' me. I ain't leavin' you either, and I swear I'm clean. Ain't wearin' a glove. Gonna come deep inside you. Fill you with it. Might make a baby. You trust me that much?"

She sucked in a breath. The idea shocked her. Not because she'd ever try to wiggle out of her commitment, but because she'd never once considered unprotected sex. It was ingrained in her, and she'd only had sex a few times. This was not only taboo, but titillating as well. And pregnant? Could she do that? If it was Stryker's baby, yeah. She could do it and love every second of it.

Her breathing came rapid, and she felt the blood rising to her cheeks as she grinned up at him. "I dare you."

Stryker barked out a laugh before reaching for her. "Oh yeah, baby. It's on."

It was like a dream. Stryker grazed his lips down her belly to her pussy. Glitter's breaths came in little pants just before he covered her with his mouth. The second he did, he flicked her clit with his tongue. She let out a sharp cry, her hands flying to his head, where she gripped his hair tightly while he groaned a deep, masculine sound of desire.

The more he licked and flicked with his tongue, the more Glitter lost control. She screamed and thrashed beneath his touch, needing more but unable to articulate what she wanted. Stryker sucked and licked her pussy until she thought she might die from the sheer desire he built so effortlessly within her. When she thought she'd reached her limit, he climbed up her body, covering her with his much larger frame. His muscles danced beneath her frantic fingers as she clawed and gripped his skin, needing more from him. Needing it all.

"You ready for me?" His fingers probed her entrance carefully, but didn't sink too deeply inside her. "You wet?"

"You know I am! Why won't you fuck me?"

"'Cause I want you so desperate for me you can't see straight. Want my cock to be the first thing I put inside that tight little body. You're gonna feel me and know you're mine."

"Do it!" Glitter was past caring if she was begging him or if he cared that she was inexperienced. "Fuck me, you bastard!"

With a little chuckle, Stryker kissed her, thrusting his tongue inside her mouth at the same time he surged forward with his hips. He took her deeply, holding himself still once he was inside her. Glitter's pussy quivered, and she knew that if he'd just pull back and thrust again, she'd come. But he didn't. Instead, he continued to kiss her over and over, nipping her bottom lip a couple of times. When he did retreat, the thrust home was harder. The third time, harder still. Always he held himself inside her for several seconds before continuing.

She was losing it. That maddening orgasm was just that little bit out of reach. Glitter tried to meet his thrusts with her own, but he gripped her hip with one hand in a punishing grip. Had she not been so completely out of control she might have told him he was hurting her. Instead she reveled in the slight pain. It meant he was nearly as out of control as she was because Stryker was always aware of what he was doing. She'd been around long enough to have seen the women he'd been with. They'd come into Beach Fit talking about him. She knew because she drank in every single thing she could. Stryker didn't do anything he didn't mean to do. But he'd never hurt her. Not ever. Not for any reason. So the bruising grip he had on her hips now wasn't meant to hurt. It was meant for him to keep control of the situation.

"Please, Stryker," she begged him on a whisper. "Please make me come. I can't stand much more!"

"Fuckin' hell," he murmured. "You're such a hot little thing! Can't move too much or I'll come."

"Then do it! We've got all day and night and the next day! Please, Stryker! Oh, God! Please!"

"Goddamn motherfuck!"

Then he moved, riding her hard. Long, powerful strokes that pushed Glitter over the edge. The second her pussy started to spasm, Stryker threw his head back and roared to the ceiling. His hot cum bathed her insides in a fiery sensation, filling her. Marking her as his. She swore she could feel each jet of seed spurting inside her. Sweat covered them both.

Glitter clung to Stryker, not wanting to let go. Not even after he collapsed his full weight on top of her. It should have felt smothering, but she loved it. She liked being pinned by him into the mattress. Then he rolled to his side, taking her with him. He looked into her eyes for long, long moments. Stroking her cheek tenderly, he brushed a damp tendril of hair off her face.

"You OK, baby?"

"I'm wonderful." She looked up into his sea-green eyes. In that moment, she thought she understood what it was like to be completely and utterly mesmerized by someone. She couldn't look away from him if she'd wanted to. He must have been content, too, because he just held her like that, stroking her hair and cheek. Letting their hearts slow after the wild ride.

"You understood what I was sayin', right? 'Cause this is done, baby. Ain't lettin' you go. Ain't lettin' you walk. Damned sure ain't lettin' another man take you away from me. I'll protect you with my life, but you took me on with the intention of me being the dominant in this relationship. That's exactly what you're gettin'."

She nodded. "I understand."

"Ain't gonna be easy sometimes, babe. There's gonna be times I expect you to obey me without question. No room for negotiation."

"I'll have to get used to it, Stryker. But I promise I'll do my best to let you take over."

"I'll try not to suffocate you, but ain't guaranteein' I won't."

"I'll try not to be the child you have to look out for."

He grinned. "Honey, I know a little about your background. Some from what you told me. Other things from stuff the club's found out over the years. Ain't sure you've ever been a child, and that's probably the problem. I'm a bastard and I admit it. But I'll be makin' most of the decisions from now on. You'll get your say in some things, but my nature is to control my environment as much as possible. That includes you now. I'll definitely be in control in the bedroom, so don't even think about withholding sex from me." He gave her a stern look but ruined it with his lips twitching, fighting a grin.

She laughed. "As if I'd deny myself the pleasure." She reached up to stroke his beard several times. "I've never experienced anything like that. Maybe it was it was the anticipation, but I think you could have done anything in the world to me and I'd have loved it."

"Anticipation?" He looked affronted, raising his eyebrows. "Baby, I'm just that good."

She burst out laughing and he pulled her to him, once again wrapping those big, strong arms around her. Stryker kissed her. Slow, languid sweeps of his tongue made her sigh with pleasure. Her pussy twitched in anticipation, but Stryker gave a long, regretful sigh.

"Ain't nothin' more I wanna do than fuck you again, but once is enough until you've had a chance to heal a little. Besides, you gonna keep up with my demands in bed, you need your strength. Which means I need to feed you." He helped her off the bed and swatted her ass lightly. "Go. Clean up. You need me, holler out. Get dressed and we'll go to the diner down the street from the club."

"Oh! Tito's?"

"Where else? Ain't fancy, but I know the food's good, and you'll eat it. Serious about you keepin' up your strength." He winked at her.

It took ten minutes for Glitter to clean up and dress. A couple of the lacerations on her back stung a little, but nothing horrible. The rest were fading from an angry red to a dull shade of pink. Only one needed a bandage, and even it showed signs of healing. Really, she felt much better than she'd thought she would.

* * *

It had only been a few weeks, but already Glitter could see many perks of being Stryker's woman. Obviously the sex was awesome, but he also treated her decently. No. Not just decently. That was an understatement. He was so careful with her, so patient. There were times he was firm with her, unbending as an oak. But he tempered that with love and care. He was continually touching her, as she'd discovered over the weeks since he'd taken her home. He either held her hand or had his arm draped around her shoulders whenever they were together. Not just when they were in public or around other people at the club. When they were alone, he would pull her down on his lap as she walked by, causing her to squeal with delight. He would drop a kiss on her cheek or the top of her head frequently. Sometimes he would give her a chaste kiss on the mouth. Other times... yeah. More than once his kisses turned hot at the clubhouse. At first, his brothers gave him a hard time, but they all praised her for taking him in hand. Some would wink at her, but none of them ever made her uncomfortable. The one time a prospect had jokingly told Stryker he wanted his turn, Stryker had punched him so hard they'd had to call in Blade to make sure Stryker hadn't done any permanent damage.

They spent a lot of time at the clubhouse, but when he was in the mood for an all-night sex fest -- which was often -- he took her to his house. There, he said she could scream as long and loud as she wanted, and no one could hear her. He'd started doing that after he'd figured out she was sometimes uncomfortable with the club girls hearing her.

He'd claimed Glitter in front of his club, but he'd ordered her vest with the property patch special, and it wasn't yet done. The club girls, though they knew better, took that to mean it wasn't a done deal. Part of Glitter was thrilled when Stryker looked down his nose at them, asking more than one, "Why would I want you when I have Glitter?" Another part felt sorry for them. She certainly wouldn't want to be compared to another woman. She'd hate the woman and be hurt by the man's words. So she'd tried to keep a low profile. Which Stryker had noticed and put a stop to. He'd simply found places for them to fuck where she'd be out of earshot and had refrained from going to the club when there were parties. Glitter had a feeling that would end the second he put his property patch on her.

Today, he and several of the brothers who had ol' ladies with them at Tito's Diner. They were all having a late supper. It was nearly dark, yet no one seemed in a hurry to leave. It was like they were waiting for something, but weren't overly concerned about it.

After a burger and a hot fudge banana shake, Glitter felt like she'd swallowed a grapefruit. She was stuffed and sleepy. Stryker had his arm around her, like usual, and leaned in to kiss her cheek affectionately. "Sleepy?"

"I'm pleasantly stuffed," she declared, rubbing her belly. "You keep feeding me like this, and I'll be in no shape to dance anywhere. I'll be sitting in a recliner expecting you to wait on me hand and foot."

The women chuckled while the men groaned. "Don't give Lucy those ideas," Vicious said with a grimace. "She already has me wrapped around her fuckin' finger."

Lucy grinned. "As if you've not been trying to get me to do just that since we found out I was pregnant."

The big, tattooed man rubbed the back of his neck as the other brothers laughed. "Yeah, well, you've had the mornin' sickness. You need to keep up your strength."

"Honey, every woman has morning sickness."

"Not me," Alizay said. "I've not been sick at all."

Beast sat up, not looking as lazy as he once had. "Blood? You fucker. You knock her up?"

Blood puffed out his chest, pulling Ali closer to him, brushing a kiss on the top of her head even as he rubbed her belly softly. "Damned straight. Pretty close to the first time too. My little guys are strong swimmers."

The men hooted with laughter while Fleur, Lucy, and Glitter congratulated Ali. The laughter had just started to die down when a big SUV pulled up to the diner. That must have been what the guys were waiting for, because they immediately waved over to Marge to settle up.

"You guys bring these lovely ladies back soon," Marge insisted. "Been too long since you acted like a family. With so many little ones on the way, me and Elena gotta insist."

"My Elena will be angry if you boys don't do as Marge says," Tito warned.

"No house specials!" Elena's voice came from the back, obviously meaning business. She poked her head around the corner, shaking her finger at the bikers. "I'll be highly offended if it's another two weeks before I see any of you again."

"Don't you worry, Elena," Fleur said. "We'll make sure they bring us at least once a week. Look after Tito for us, will you?"

"Now, don't you be looking to take my man, young lady."

"And don't you be looking to take mine," Lucy said with a giggle. "Tito still believes he'll lose you to one of the boys."

"It's a sad truth," Tito said, looking as dejected as a man could look. He still winked at Lucy. "One of these wicked, wicked boys will run off with my woman, and I'll be left in sorrow."

"Ah, Tito," Elena said grinning at her husband's dramatics. "You know no one can rock the boat for me the way you can." She blew a kiss to him. Tito pretended to catch it and put it over his heart.

"And you, my dear, are the woman of my heart. Not even such beautiful women as these could compare to me in your eyes."

"Stop trying so hard to get laid, Tito," Stryker grumbled.

"Yeah," Beast said as he handed Marge a few bills. "You're makin' the rest of us look bad."

The girl giggled while the other men pretended to be put out, all the while urging the women toward the door.

Once outside, the men from Salvation's Bane escorted the women to the SUV and kissed them as they helped them inside.

"What's going on?" The whole thing struck Glitter as wrong. "What's happening? I want to ride with you."

"Lock's gonna take you all back to the clubhouse. Got business to attend to."

A sudden thought hit Glitter and she had to know. "You're going to the Dark. Aren't you?"

"Babe, you knew we couldn't ignore it forever."

"But why didn't you tell me sooner?"

"Wouldn't have told you at all, but I won't ever lie to you. Keep that in mind when you ask me something you may not want to know."

"I'm not fragile, Stryker. I can handle this. I just want to know when you're doing something dangerous."

"So you can worry over me?"

"Isn't that what women do? I can't go with you, so I'll worry about you until you get back."

He pulled her into his arms and kissed her gently for several seconds, then rested his forehead against hers. "I didn't tell you because I didn't want you to worry. I'll be fine. I have my brothers, with more on the way. We got each other's backs."

"Yeah, Glitter," Havoc called from his bike next to the SUV. "We won't let him singe one hair on his pretty little head."

"Or his ass," Beast added.

"I brought the bubble wrap, sweetie," Tobias said. "If he can't survive with all that, he ain't good enough for ya." He winked at her while Stryker flipped him off. "Speaking of. You decide you want an upgrade, I'm your man, princess. Anything Stryker can do, I can do better."

Glitter couldn't help but laugh at the nonsense, knowing it was their way of putting her at ease. "I'll do you one better. You guys don't bring him back in one piece, I'll tell Marge. See how you like it with no Marge special shakes."

A collective groan went up before Thorn chuckled, starting his bike and revving it. The sign it was time to go. Stryker helped her inside the SUV then kissed her through the window. "I'll be wantin' to fuck when I get back."

"Shocker," she said with a grin. "Since you always want to fuck."

He winked, then climbed on his own bike, started it, and followed his brothers into the night.

Chapter Seven

The Dark club, like the last time he was there, gave Stryker a sense of foreboding. Evil. The place wasn't a legitimate meeting place for people in the lifestyle to gather and play in a safe environment. That was a fact. Again, when he and his brothers entered, there were women who didn't seem to want to be there, but didn't cry for help. Making sure they got out was Blade's top priority. The rest of them were there for vengeance and to send a fucking message.

"Blade, you've got twenty minutes and counting. Get anyone out who doesn't want to die." Thorn was no nonsense about this when Stryker wanted to go medieval on everyone.

"This place is an abomination," Tobias muttered as he readied himself. "Good riddance if you ask me."

"Not till I say," Thorn warned. "We do this just as we outlined. Twenty minutes."

They fanned out in pairs. All the members of Salvation's Bane but a handful of trustworthy prospects and a couple of key members. Fortunately, Bones MC had joined the party at the clubhouse, and Thorn felt free to take the bulk of his club away for business. Such was the beauty of sister clubs.

"You guys got a lot of fuckin' nerve comin' here." A skinny guy who looked no more than twenty-five or -six strode up to them. He carried a rifle, resting the barrel on his shoulder as he approached them. Three more men were at his back, all of them older and armed. Stryker studied them all, picking out his targets like he knew his brothers were doing. They were all connected with radio comms and throat mics so it was easy to tell what was going on with each small group.

So far, the explosives setup was going according to plan with no one interfering.

Thorn rested his hand on the gun at his hip. "And you guys got a lot of fuckin' nerve settin' up a shitshow like this in my fuckin' town. And don't think I don't know about the drugs. I know everything."

The guy smirked and chuckled, looking at his buddies for shared amusement. They all just looked at each other, shifting nervously. "You don't know shit, motherfucker. Kiss of Death is the new club in town. You can't handle a little competition? Get the fuck outta the way."

Thorn tilted his head, seeming to consider the situation. "What's your name, boy?"

"Horse," he chuckled, looking back at his buddies. "'Cause I'm hung like a --"

"Yeah, a horse. I get it." Then under his breath, Thorn muttered, "Lame-ass motherfucker."

"Yeah? Why don't you do something about it, old man."

"You get one chance at this, kid. Where's your president?"

"Fuck you! Waste 'em!"

Before the four men could so much as point their weapons, Stryker and Thorn had shot three of them. The third one -- the kid -- pulled the trigger to his rifle but nothing happened. With a yell, he charged them, swinging with the barrel of his weapon. Stryker caught it, yanked it free of his hands, then stepped in and headbutted the little bastard. Kid sank to the floor, where Blood zip-tied his hands behind his back. He did the same to his ankles and tied them to his wrists, effectively hogtying the kid. Blood was already in the process of cleaning up the kills, bagging the bodies and washing up the blood with bleach. They planned on torching the place, but Blood didn't leave anything to chance.

"You motherfuckers!" the kid yelled, his face an angry shade of purple. "You're all gonna fuckin' die! You and the bitch you stole!"

Stryker knelt in front of him, pulling his head back by his hair. "Where's Butcher?"

"Go fuck yourself!"

Stryker pulled out his knife, examined the tip of it, and then, in a move so quick the kid had no idea what was coming, sliced off his ear. Immediately, Stryker pulled Horse's head to him, petting his hair and crooning to him like he was trying to soothe a child. "Shh, shh. Now there. It's all over. That's it. Shhhh."

"You cocksucker! Ahh! Ahh! Motherfucker!"

"You said that already. Now, just calm down. Take a deep breath. In, then out. Shh... It's all right. It's all right." Stryker was laying it on thick, but he needed specific information. This Horse character was probably the best way of getting it. He was young enough he would want to impress and move up in the ranks of his club. The president might have actually given him a position of authority since the gunmen behind him had been under his lead.

It took the kid a few precious minutes to finally get himself under control. When he did, Stryker praised him. "That's good. Very good. You did well, Horse. Now," he shifted his position just a little, resting the blade of his knife casually on his leg. "I need to know where Rat Man and Butcher are. You tell me that, and that's it. I'll let you go. You'll get out of here and go on your way. No one will know anything. Just tell me where Rat Man and Butcher are." Horse's eyes rolled wildly, as if he were looking for someone in particular. "Don't worry. Ain't no one around but us." When Horse kept looking around them, Stryker smacked his face just enough to sting and bring the kid's attention back to him. "Rat Man. Butcher. Where are they, kid?"

"B-Butcher is... h-he's in the b-back. Watchin' the g-girls on the cams."

"Makin' sure they're doin' their jobs?"

"I -- n-no. Makin' sure they don't try to g-get someone t-to help them leave."

"That's good, Horse. You done real good." Again, he praised the kid, like he might a dog. "Now. One more. Rat Man. Where's Rat Man?"

At the mention of the president's name, Horse seemed to summon up his courage. Stryker could see the stubbornness flash in his eyes, and knew there was no way to get the information quickly. He looked back at Thorn, who glanced at his watch.

"We got time." That was code for Stryker to continue with the torture. Which he gladly did.

This time, Stryker brought up the blade slowly. The kid started to whimper. Sweat soaked his skin, beading on his forehead. His eyes locked on the large knife Stryker held, his breathing erratic. "You don't want to go through this for that bastard, Horse. He's not worth it. Save yourself some pain. Just tell me where Rat Man is."

Horse shook his head and whimpered, his gaze never leaving the knife. Stryker raised it slowly, moving toward the kid's face. Horse's breathing increased until he was practically panting. Whimpers and stifled cries came through the puffs of breath. With each exhalation, the kid blew saliva from his mouth in heavy puffs.

Stryker left no doubt where he was headed with the tip of that knife. Slowly, inch by inch, the tip moved ever closer to his left eye. Finally, the blade rested just below it, lying on Horse's cheek. The kid was shaking now, crying out with every breath he took.

"All you gotta do is tell me, kid. You can stop it now. Just tell me where to find Rat Man."

"No!" Horse's voice was more a guttural grunt than a forceful denial, but it was clear either the kid was completely loyal to Rat Man, or more scared of his president than he was Stryker.

"Suit yourself." To the sounds of Horse's high-pitched screams, Stryker pierced the kid's eyeball with the tip of his knife and flicked it out. Blood gushed both from where Stryker's knife sank into the globe and where the eye was ripped traumatically from the socket. It hung there, swinging by the optic nerve with every move Horse made.

This time, Stryker let him scream and stayed crouched before him with that knife at the ready. Follow-through was the mother of intimidation.

When Horse had passed the point where the pain overrode his awareness of the situation, Stryker spoke again. "Rat Man."

"He'll kill me, man!" Horse was crying now, pleading.

"He ain't here. I am. Rat Man."

"He's s-supposed to be m-meeting with a c-club i-in Lake Worth."

"Goddamned mother-fuck," Thorn swore softly, a rare show of anger during an operation. "Fuckin' Black Reign."

"You're sure it was Lake Worth?" Stryker focused squarely on his prey. "Lake Worth. Black Reign."

"That's the name of the club. They wanted to talk about the drugs Kiss of Death's been movin'."

"You know why they wanted the meeting?"

Horse shook his head. "Rat Man said he thought they was wantin' to help us."

Stryker knew that, with El Diablo, help wasn't likely the scenario. More likely he was looking to get his share of the pie.

A commotion came over the radio. Several calls at once made for confusion. "Everyone calm the fuck down. Havoc. Report."

"Black Reign's joined the party. I got fuckin' Rycks and Shotgun with me."

"They makin' a threat?"

"No. Not at present."

"Thorn. El Segador. We need to talk."

"The bloody Reaper," Stryker muttered. "What the fuck's he doin' here?"

"What's Black Reign's interest?"

"Shutting down this operation." Like his counterpart, El Diablo, El Segador was eloquent and neatly spoken with a slight British accent.

"You'll understand if I call bullshit." Thorn didn't hesitate.

"Of course. It's not what most clubs would do, but I can assure you, we have no interest in another one-percent club setting up shop. We also take exception to them cutting into our business."

Thorn looked at Stryker. It was the only way the president of Salvation's Bane ever indicated he wanted an opinion. "I don't trust them, but Reign's not been actively trying to kill us. Besides, El Diablo isn't a pussy. He wants a club dead, he'll cut off the head himself. Not send a flunky, no matter how qualified the flunky."

Thorn gave him a short nod. Then spoke. "West corner. You've got five minutes. In eight minutes, the place is gone." There was no reply, but then Stryker didn't expect there would be. Neither did Thorn. "Havoc. Check the back. Probably the security station. If Butcher's there, bring him."

"Rest of the place is secure. Got three more groups of four. All of them appear to be either low-level patches or prospects. Ain't no Kiss of Death worth killin' here."

"Understood. Clear the building. We'll follow in four." El Segador, Rycks, and Shotgun approached them just as Thorn finished his instructions.

"Wasn't expecting to find Bane here," El Segador said as he stopped in front of Thorn. "I take it you have a problem with Kiss of Death as well?"

"This club is an abomination," Thorn growled. "That's enough. But, since you brought it up, this is our town. No club runs drugs or anything else through it without comin' to us first."

"As it should be."

"Why'd you invite their president to Black Reign for a chat?"

El Segador shrugged. "Who knows what El Diablo has in mind? I can assure you it's not to join with this filth." He frowned as he looked around them. "Anyone who would take something beautiful and turn it into… this, deserves to die."

"El Diablo plannin' on killin' the bastard?"

"As I said. I cannot speak to El Diablo's plans regarding Rat Man. They're his own. I can, however, assure you Black Reign is still firmly out of your business. While we do have concerns with what Kiss of Death was doing here, we've made certain assurances to both Salvation's Bane and Bones not to conduct any business in your territories. El Diablo is many things, but he's a man of his word."

"I'm supposed to just believe that?" Thorn shifted his weight, readying himself to pull his gun if necessary. Stryker had already sheathed his knife and switched off the safety to his gun.

"Believe it, or not. It's the truth. You have sources who can verify our movement. Check with them."

"I'll be doin' that. Why you here?"

"I suspect the same thing you're doing here. I have every intention of destroying this club and any members of Kiss of Death left in the area alive."

"Sounds like most of them scuttled off," Stryker commented. "They with their president?"

"They are. My instructions were to send a message here. After that, if they persist, we'll clean house."

"There's a man they call Butcher," Stryker said. "If he's in Lake Worth, I want him alive."

El Segador grinned. "My, my. Is that a favor being asked?"

Stryker wanted to kill the motherfucker right there. When he stepped forward, Thorn shot him a quelling look.

"It's not," Thorn said. "It's Stryker claimin' the kill on the man who tortured his woman."

Instantly, El Segador's demeanor changed. Gone was the polite gentleman. In his place was the man's namesake. *El Segador. The Reaper.* "Of course. I'll notify El Diablo immediately. If the man is in our clubhouse, he'll soon be in your custody." Every man with El

Segador had gone into what Stryker liked to call kill mode. He'd been there for some time himself. So had Thorn. Now, they were all united in one purpose. Kill every last son of a bitch in this club.

"Any innocents left in this fuckin' place?" Thorn asked over the radio.

"All the girls are out," Blade responded. "None of the men seemed to have survived the night."

"Good. Blood? You got things covered?"

"Team's bagging the last up now," he said, briefly consulting the men he had helping him. "Only thing I'm waitin' on is Horse. He stayin' or goin'?"

Stryker pulled his weapon. Before Horse could do anything more than whimper, Stryker shot him in the head. "Stayin'."

"I'll need two minutes," Blood said, not wasting time. Three other members of Bane helped him as the rest of the brothers made their way to the entrance of the club.

"T-minus three minutes. Anyone not wantin' to be inside when this thing goes, better get the fuck out now."

True to his word, two minutes later, Blood and his team appeared. They all got on their bikes and headed out. With a little help from Data at Bones, city cameras had been disrupted for several blocks, ensuring they made a clean getaway. They were six blocks away when the building exploded. None of them looked back.

Chapter Eight

The night seemed to creep along at a snail's pace. The ol' ladies were wonderful and did their best to distract her, but they were on edge too. Seemed she wasn't the only one who didn't like being left behind.

"Don't worry so much," Lucy said. "The men can take care of themselves." She seemed to be trying to convince herself as much as she was the other women. "They'll be fine."

"How often do you manage to convince yourself of that, Lucy?" Fleur said with a grin.

"Not a damned time."

They all giggled nervously.

"No matter how many times they do something like this, I never relax until they're all home safely." Lucy took a sip of her drink, for the first time looking as nervous as Glitter felt.

"Well, I'm just glad I'm not the only one," Glitter said. "How often does it happen?"

Mariana stood and came to Glitter, putting a hand on her shoulder. "Not often. And always for a good reason. They aren't saints, but they protect their women, their club, and their community. Apparently, Kiss of Death threatened all of that."

"Which means," Lucy continued, "Bane won't go easy on them."

"Good," Glitter muttered. "Fuckers are crazy."

"I'm just thankful Stryker and Tobias got you out of there when they did," Spring, Havoc's woman, commented. "Havoc said Stryker told him the Dark was nothing short of a house of torture."

"It was." Glitter rubbed her arms. Chills coursed through her at the memory. She'd wanted a taste of the forbidden and had bitten off more than she could chew. She looked out the window at the road in front of the clubhouse, hoping to see the guys pull in safe and sound, but it had been hours.

There was a knock at the door to Mariana and Thorn's room where they'd all holed up. Lucy was closest to the door, so she answered it to find one of the club girls lazily draped against the frame. She took her time straightening, her gaze boldly meeting Lucy's before dropping, a little grin curling her lips. "Might wanna turn on the news. Been some problems with our boys across town."

Lucy gave a little gasp, but Fleur was at her side. "Easy, sister. Go sit down and I'll sort this out." Alizay and Mariana helped Lucy to the couch, soothing her as they went.

"I'm sure there's nothing to worry about, Lucy. Just take a deep breath." From what Glitter understood, the pregnancy was hard on her, but she was fighting as best she could. Blade assured her that pregnancy affected every woman differently and to just roll with it. He'd added that if Thorn didn't coddle her properly to give him a call and Blade would beat some manners into Thorn.

Glitter stood beside Fleur. The other woman gave the club girl a venomous look. "I know some of you have your eye on Thorn, Beast, and several of the men who've taken ol' ladies, but Vicious is not leaving Lucy. None of them are leaving us. Keep treating the ol' ladies like this, and as wife of the enforcer of Salvation's Bane, I'll take matters into my own hands."

Glitter knew the woman from Beach Fit. Her name was Ritta, and she'd had her mind set on locking down either the president or vice president of Salvation's Bane since Glitter had first arrived. Neither man had realized, or if they did, they didn't care.

They'd made their choices and couldn't be happier. Ritta, on the other hand, hadn't accepted reality.

"Ain't nothin' you can do. Little thing like you." She looked Fleur up and down as if sizing her up and finding her lacking.

Fleur lashed out, slamming the heel of her hand into Ritta's nose with more force than Glitter thought possible for such a small woman. Glitter reacted before she could think. When Ritta would have struck back, Glitter struck out the same as Fleur. Like all the dancers in Salvation's Angels, she'd had basic self-defense, and the move was instinctive. Heel of the hand to the nose or upward into the chin. Blood splattered around her hand, but Fleur didn't stop. She pulled her arm back and did it again. And again. And again.

Glitter didn't have to do anything else other than bear witness.

Finally, Ritta slumped down the wall and didn't get up. Breathing hard and looking angrier than Glitter had ever seen one of the ol' ladies, Fleur pulled out her cell. She pressed a button and put the phone to her ear. "Lock. Ritta is outside Thorn and Anna's room. I want her out of the compound."

"You can't do that," Ritta mumbled. "Only the president can expel someone."

"Yeah? He ain't here. And you just distressed his pregnant wife. I'm making an executive decision. So fuck off!"

Glitter raised an eyebrow at Fleur. "That was… excessive?"

Fleur shrugged. "PMS."

They headed inside, not waiting to see if Lock did as Fleur told him.

"What is it?" Glitter and Fleur headed to the TV where the other women had gathered. On the local news, they saw a massive fire across town at a "local club." According to the reporter, there was no indication as to the source of the catastrophic explosion that caused windows to be blown out for two blocks and the massive fire that consumed the building. Investigations were underway. And a search inside the club was currently impossible. No one was found near the club, and it was unknown if there was anyone inside.

"Oh, God," Alizay said, sinking down beside Lucy. "Blood."

The door to the room opened. "Ahh, I think they missed us." Beast's voice boomed as the women all jumped and ran to the men entering the room. Fleur threw herself into Beast's arms, kissing him soundly before pulling back and slapping him full on the face.

"Fucker!" she screamed at him. "Do you know what seeing that did to me?" She gestured to the TV and the images of the burning building.

"Oww! The fuck?"

"If I didn't like your cock so much, I'd nut you right here, you bastard!"

"Easy, woman! Easy! I'm fine. We're fine! We're all fine!"

"You better be glad," Fleur said. "'Cause if you'd been dead, I'd have killed you!" Then she burst into tears.

Glitter was trembling, but she refused to let herself break down. The others could. They were all established with their men, and some were pregnant. It was allowed. She was still so new to the group. A group she wasn't sure she belonged in.

Stryker found her the second he walked into the room. His gaze met hers, and he opened his arms. Unable to stop herself, Glitter ran into them, throwing herself into his arms and hugging him fiercely. "I was so scared," she whimpered. "I was so scared!"

"No need to worry, honey. Brothers got my back. I got theirs."

There was quiet sobbing throughout the room. Fleur was no exception, but continued to pummel Beast.

"That's one serious case of PMS, Fleur." Mariana giggled as she pushed out of her man's arms and went to her friend. She pulled Fleur into her arms and hugged her until the other woman calmed down. All the ol' ladies gathered around Fleur and spoke softly to her, bringing her into the circle of their warmth and love. Glitter wanted to be there so bad. But she couldn't bring herself to leave Stryker.

Then Mariana glanced over at her and smiled. She motioned to her, beckoning her to come to them. At first Glitter was confused. Then Mariana gave her a grin and a little exasperated sigh, walked to her and took her hand.

"Get over here with us. We can't forgive them this easily, and you need us the same as we need you. Besides. If I know our men, they caused the explosion. Which means we'll have to figure out a way to help the innocent bystanders who got their windows demolished." She gave her man a reproachful look before turning back to the sisterhood of bikers' women in the room.

Stryker kissed the top of her head before urging her to go with Mariana. Once in the circle of women, she let the tears flow.

* * *

Seeing Glitter take her place with his brothers' women warmed Stryker's heart. They were making her feel welcome, and she was fitting in nicely, if Lock could be believed. Sounded like Glitter had joined in with Fleur to give a club girl a beating. Apparently, the girl had been all too happy to upset Lucy and deliver what she saw as bad news with less than a delicate touch.

Now, all the men were grumbling and trying to get their women away from each other so they could have some quiet time. Stryker had intended on heading to Lake Worth to interrogate that bastard Butcher. Unfortunately, he hadn't shown at the Black Reign clubhouse, nor had Rat Man. Which meant Glitter was right. There was someone on the inside feeding another club information. Fortunately, Thorn knew who it was and had taken care of the problem. Permanently. Prospect named Gojo had been selling drugs with Tanya out of Salvation's Angels. When he used more than he could pay for -- which Kiss of Death had known he'd do -- they'd demanded he pay them in information. Kiss of Death had known every move Salvation's Bane had made over the space of about a month and a half. There were things Thorn would have preferred Kiss of Death not know, but nothing he considered catastrophic. All in all, Stryker figured they were lucky. It could have been a lot worse.

Butcher and Rat Man were in the wind. Probably on the way back to Nashville, but Stryker could bide his time. Eventually, they'd get the sons of bitches. Right now, he had other things to worry about. Like the naked woman currently handcuffed to his bed. Instead of a gag, he'd chosen to blindfold her. Just this once. He knew he'd not be able to last long though. He wanted to watch her eyes as she stared into his when she came.

"Such a beautiful sight," he purred. Glitter lay spread eagle, naked and glistening with sweat. Her breath came in little gasps with every lash of his tongue on her body. He hadn't yet tasted her pussy. That was for later. Right now, he was licking, and nipping, and kissing all the other exquisite parts of her.

"You're doing this on purpose," she gasped. "Keeping me on the edge."

"Of course," he said, chuckling around one ripe nipple. "It will be worth it when I let you come."

"Oh, God!"

She strained against the padded cuffs he'd put her in. Not once had she looked at him with trepidation, just did what he told her without question. Immediately. She'd looked at him so trustingly he'd hated covering her eyes, but he knew the lack of sensation would make it so much better for her.

Arching her back, Glitter offered her breast to him, straining to find his mouth. He raked his tongue over her pebbled nipples over and over. One. Then the other. Her narrow rib cage and tucked-in waist beckoned for his touch. He loved the feel of her silky skin beneath his rough palms. Running his hands up and down her sides to her breasts was a pleasure he never intended to deny himself.

"So fuckin' beautiful," he said. "And you're all mine."

"Yes!" she yelled out when he bit down on her nipple. "More! Please, Stryker! More!"

"That's my girl," he crooned. "So fuckin' responsive. So fuckin' lovely."

She pulled against her cuffs, straining a little before relaxing again. She did it each time he pulled her back from the brink. Stryker loved the little sounds she made as she struggled to come and when he stopped her from coming. Which he did over and over.

"Here, Stryker," she panted, trying to bend her knees, spreading her legs as far as she could. "My pussy! Please! My pussy!" The cuffs clattered where he'd fastened them to the wooden head- and footboards. She was beginning to strain hard against them now. He had to wonder how much she was getting ready to resist her bonds when he ate her pussy for the next hour.

Thirty minutes later, he got his answer. Glitter's body was covered in sweat, her hair plastered to her head and face. She screamed with every lash of his tongue.

"Finish me, you bastard!" Her demand was at the top of her lungs.

"Now, where would be the fun in that?"

He turned on a small vibrator. The sound was a soft, low hum. The second he turned it on, she cocked her head.

"What's that? Stryker? What is that?"

"Just a little toy to play with. Maybe I'll make you my toy from now on."

With just the lightest of touches, he traced the tapered tip of the vibrator around the hood of her clit. Barely there. Never touching where she needed most.

"Oh, God! Oh, God!"

"Oh, no, baby. This ain't God. This is all me." His sweet, cajoling tone turned hard. "Say my name, Glitter."

"Stryker," she whispered, thrusting her hips at him, no doubt in an attempt to make him put that vibrator on her clit.

"Louder."

"Stryker!"

"That's my good girl. You wanna come?"

"Yes! Fuck yes! Make me come!"

He chuckled. "You gotta say please, baby."

"Please!" She screamed the word.

"Say, pretty please."

"Pretty please! God, Stryker! Just let me fucking come already!"

"Say... pretty please with sugar on it."

"Fucker!" She had to be screaming at the top of her lungs now. Her skin was so damp with sweat the bed sheets were wet with it. She was so turned on, her pussy glistened with her moisture. She was more than ready for him. Stryker had done this a long time. He'd played with women at the club, in the clubhouse -- there had even been one or two he'd hooked up with more than once. But never at his house. And never had there been a woman so desperate for him to fuck her.

He stood, removing his clothing. Giving his cock a lazy stroke, he removed Glitter's blindfold. She blinked several times, shaking her head to get her vision back. Always, her head turned to him. It took her eyes time to focus, but she always looked to him.

When he stood over her, his cock in his hand and a shit-eating grin on his face, she bared her teeth and yelled at him. Like a little angry badger, she screamed her frustration.

Stryker couldn't help himself. He chuckled. His cock throbbed. Ached.

"You know, I could finish myself with one stroke. Come all over you."

"Don't you dare..."

"It'd let me last longer the next time," he said, pondering just how pissed she'd be if he did it.

"I'm not gonna last any longer! What the fuck, Stryker!"

"Now, now, baby. You're meant to be my sub. That means I call the shots."

"I take it back! I don't wanna be a sub anymore! Now fuck me!"

"Such a demanding little thing." He grinned, stroking his cock once and gritting his teeth to keep from coming. He loved this demanding side of her. The little bite to her voice. The way she was so giving with her emotions. In this moment, Stryker was certain she'd happily kill him if she had the chance. Well. After she'd fucked him, of course. "I think you need to learn a lesson all subs have to learn at some point."

"Stryker," she said warningly.

"You're not in control here, baby." He gripped his shaft in a firmer grip and gave one hard stroke. Then another. "I am." Then Stryker threw back his head and roared his release. Cum shot from his dick like a fountain. She screamed her displeasure as his seed streaked her body in one hot lash after another. It was the only time he'd ever lash her lovely, pale skin. He'd whipped women before when it was mutually consented. And he wasn't above spanking her ass red with his hand, but he'd never whip her. There was no way he could get any kind of pleasure in making her look like she had when he'd found her in the Dark. Never.

"You asshole!" She half yelled at him, half sobbed. "You fucking asshole!"

"But you look so beautiful covered in my cum. I may have to do it several times before I fuck you."

"Stryker... So help me God, I will get untied from here. When I do, you won't be so smug."

"Yeah. I'm sure I'll have a fight on my hands. Heard about what you and Fleur did to poor Ritta. Is that the kind of behavior I can expect from my ol' lady from here on out?"

Glitter tried to sit up, but the cuffs on her wrists prevented it. "Look. That bitch had it coming. She was being mean to Lucy. And I didn't start it. I just had Fleur's back."

"You misunderstand me, baby. I ain't upset with you. It kinda turned me on."

She looked at him like he'd lost his mind. "Me assaulting one of the club girls… turns you on?"

"Hell, yeah. You fought with my brother's woman. You stand with them when they need you. Baby, I couldn't be prouder."

"Then why the fuck aren't you fucking me? You know, rewarding me for being a good little girl?"

"Oh, no, baby. You're a very, very naughty little submissive."

"I think we've established the fact that I'm not exactly a submissive. I thought I needed it…" She trailed off, looking confused. Which wouldn't do.

"Look at me, Glitter," he said, all teasing gone from his voice. He was deadly serious. "What you described to me is exactly a submissive. You're not just submissive in bed when I play with you hard. Sometimes you need to be submissive out of bed. Which is where I come in. It suits me better. My personality and my position with the club means I can't tolerate having to explain myself every time I give you an order. And I'll be giving orders, make no mistake. Until we catch this Butcher guy and Rat Man, I'm not going to lighten up when we're not in the safety of the club." He sighed, getting between her legs slowly so he sat with her thighs draped over his. "In bed, Glitter, I need this wildcat. This woman who's vocal about what she wants. I pushed you just to see what would happen. And believe me, baby, I'm gonna do it over and over again. Every night I can manage to get these cuffs around your wrists."

"I will fuck you up."

He grinned. "There's my girl."

His dick was still leaking cum, but he was still hard as stone. Grinning at her, he leaned in and rubbed the head of his cock over her clit. Her little indrawn breath was music to his ears.

"You better finish me this time, Stryker. I'm done begging."

"God, I love you," he whispered, meaning every fucking word. "Don't ever change, Glitter. You need me to protect you from the world, to take care of you, I'll do it. But you continue to be a demanding little wench in bed."

She opened her mouth, probably to tell him to go fuck himself. But when he slid his cock inside her to the hilt, she let out a little cry instead.

Glitter was about to lose her mind. She'd had a slight reprieve while he'd explained things to her, but the second his cock had rubbed over her clit, she was right back where she'd started. Then he filled her more completely than she'd ever thought possible. The second he stopped moving, his cock hitting high inside her, her body fragmented into a huge orgasm. She screamed even as she tightened her thighs over his legs, rocking back and forth as best she could with the cuffs on her ankles, fucking herself to ride out the pleasure.

"That's it, baby. Come on my dick. Do it all you want. Do it enough, I'll reward you with my cum in your pussy."

"Oh, fuck!" She gasped and panted as Stryker slowly lowered himself atop her. Her sweat and his cum made their bodies slip and slide against each other. Every stroke of his cock inside her built the pleasure again, little by little. Her clit throbbed and ached, too sensitive for her to hold out long. Her stomach muscles bunched, and she clenched his cock as her pussy continued to contract around him.

"That's what I'm doing, baby." He winked at her. "Try to keep up."

She bared her teeth at him, leaning up to snap at his shoulder. She connected with his skin, nipping hard enough he winced.

"Witch," he hissed in her ear. "Fuckin' little witch!"

Like she'd turned on some kind of switch, Stryker adjusted his position over her and started a hard, driving rhythm. The ride was teeth clattering and so fucking erotic Glitter was sure her brain matter had been permanently tweaked. She came and came and came again. Straining against her bonds, she tried to participate, but he'd certainly known what he was doing when he'd cuffed her. She could only move enough to frustrate herself. Stryker, in the meantime, was giving her the fuck of her life.

"Fuckin' take it, Glitter," he growled. "Take my cock. Take all of it!"

"Yes! Yes! Fuck me with it! Fuck me hard!"

With a yell, Stryker did what she demanded of him. His hips snapped hard against her, driving his cock deep over and over. Again and over again. Flesh meeting flesh slapped loud in the air. His growls and snarls mingled with the slaps and Glitter's own cries and whimpers.

Finally, with one mighty thrust and a roar of completion, Stryker came inside her. Glitter loved the feel of his hot cum splashing against her inside. She screamed, and her clit dragged over his body until she dissolved, herself. The orgasm that hit her was nothing short of nuclear. Her body clamped down on his, her muscles seized, and another scream was ripped from her throat against her will.

The next thing she knew, Stryker was unfastening the cuffs and murmuring softly to her. Glitter's eyes were so heavy, her limbs the same. Somehow, Stryker was able to carry her into the bathroom. He set her on the toilet while he adjusted the water and sent a quick text. Then he carried her into the shower and just held her for long, long moments.

"Who you texting?"

"Beast. Need to get word to Fleur we need help." He gave her a soft look. "You good, baby?"

"Um hmm," she mumbled, wondering why they needed help. And from Fleur? But she was too sex-drunk to ask.

He washed her thoroughly, cleaning all the cum from her body. By the time he got her out of the shower and dried off, the bed had been changed and was clean.

"Who..."

"Fleur," Stryker said. "Maybe another of the ol' ladies. One of the perks of being in the clubhouse.

"Clubhouse," she said dumbly. Then it hit her. "Oh my God. Everyone heard us."

Stryker, the bastard, just grinned. "Unless they're deaf, I'd say that was very likely."

"I'll never be able to show my face again. The club girls will eat me alive."

Just as she finished, there was a long wail, followed by a guttural bellow.

"Don't think you got anything to worry about, baby."

Glitter lay back on the bed, exhausted and pleasantly sore. Then she started to giggle. When Stryker followed with his deep chuckle, she dissolved into laughter, turning and reaching for Stryker. He pulled her into his arms and held her. Finally at peace, Glitter fell asleep with a smile on her face, in the arms of the one man she loved with all her heart.

Chapter Nine

Surprisingly, it had taken little effort to talk Stryker into taking her to Salvation's Angels to see her friends. He'd also told her she could dance if she wanted, but it would be in her best interest to not accept tips. Tips involved touching, and he could take people looking at her, but not touching. Glitter was amazed at how happy that made her. She was really looking forward to dancing again. The tips didn't matter. Looking into the audience and seeing Stryker watching her did. It surprised her, since she understood why club members weren't allowed to be with the dancers, but she wasn't questioning it. If he couldn't handle it, she trusted him to pluck her off stage and make off with her. She grinned at the thought.

Now, she was backstage, hanging with her girls. Stryker had kissed her soundly before heading off to check the security detail for the evening. She fully expected him to be front and center when she took the stage. She found she was actually nervous. It had only been a few weeks, but she'd really missed this. Maybe she'd have to dance for Stryker in private. She was sure he wouldn't mind at all.

She'd given her music to the DJ earlier. Havoc had approved her request with a wink and a pat on her shoulder. "Missed you, Glitter. You're welcome any time Stryker feels like he can keep from killin' anyone." Glitter had laughed and hugged the man. Stryker had growled and pulled her away, giving his brother a killing look. Havoc had chuckled and moved on.

The second her music started and Glitter strutted out on stage, a sense of peace and happiness washed over her. Yeah. She loved this. Maybe it was the adrenaline. Maybe it was just the joy of dancing. But the thought of Stryker watching her while she swished her hips and shook her ass was a huge turn on. More than having the eyes of other men on her. More than all the money she could make if she were taking tips. It was all about Stryker.

And there he was. Standing at the end of the stage, watching her with hungry eyes. Glitter couldn't help but run her hands over her body like she wanted him to do. She squeezed her tits, all the while letting her hips snap side to side to the rhythm of the music. Her hair was a long mass of auburn curls that fanned out with every twirl of her body, every whip of her head.

She spun around and around, holding to the pole in the stage floor as she did. Glitter wrapped her legs around it to hold herself as her momentum carried her around twice before shifting her grip to hold the pole above her head and kick her legs up straight and spread eagle so she was bent at the waist. The pole continued to spin her around, her pussy on fine display to everyone. Glitter had no doubt it was wet in her excitement. Would Stryker notice? Would everyone else? She'd placed a jeweled clip with strands of gems that fell across her pussy when she presented it like this. She also had a jeweled plug in her ass. Something she was looking forward to having Stryker help her remove later. Her tits had jeweled clamps around her nipples, and her skin shimmered from the fine flecks of gold in the lotion she'd applied. All in all, she looked fucking hot.

The soles of her eight-inch platform heels hit the stage, and she continued to spin back up the runway to the main stage where Stryker stood looking equally turned on and murderous. She blew him a kiss to the cheers and catcalls of the men surrounding them.

On impulse, Glitter squatted down in front of Stryker, spreading her legs wide so he could have a close-up look at her decorations and glistening pussy lips. He looked her up and down hungrily, actually licking his lips. The bulge of his cock behind his jeans was impossible to ignore. Glitter wanted him with a fierceness she had no way of ignoring.

She stood slowly, beckoning him with a crook of her finger. The crowd cheered wildly as she bent over, playing with her butt plug, twisting it and pumping it slightly as she kept her eyes on Stryker. Taunting him. Teasing him. Needing him up there on that fucking stage with her like she needed to breathe.

She continued to watch Stryker as she shook her ass, pumping that plug ever so slightly in invitation. More than one man next to the stage decided it would be a good idea to join her, but all managed to be stopped by their friends. Mostly because anyone who frequented Salvation's Angels had seen this kind of show before. Dancers could invite men on the stage, but random men just hopping up there were shut down forcibly.

When his jaw clenched, so did Glitter's pussy. He was going to join her. She knew he was. She could see it in his eyes and the set of his jaw. Taking out his phone, he sent off a quick text, then climbed onto the bar running the length of the stage, then up onto the runway with her.

Stryker took her offered hand and raised it above her head, urging her to twirl for him. She did with a smile. Glitter wrapped her arms around him, turning them so her back was to the audience where they could see her. As expected, the crowd urged her on.

Running her soft hands over his wide chest, Glitter walked all around him, letting her hands wander over him as she went. When she was behind him, she slid her arms around his waist, pulling the T-shirt from his jeans and tunneling her hands underneath to slide up his torso, taking the shirt with her. Stryker gave her a "really?" look over his shoulder and just whipped the damned thing off. Glitter curled her fingers and scratched slowly down his chest from behind. She felt him rumble a groan, but the sound was covered by the cheers of the crowd. The few women in the crowd -- including the dancers and servers -- approached the stage with their drinks and cheered them on.

Strangely, in this setting, Glitter found she enjoyed knowing the women were watching Stryker. More correctly, watching her caressing Stryker. When she brushed her hand lightly down the front of his jeans, his cock twitched. So she lingered, stroking lightly. The ladies became nearly as vocal as the men. Maybe more so since they had shriller catcalls.

Hooking her thumbs in the waistband of Stryker's jeans, Glitter peeked around him, looking up at him with a grin. He just rolled his eyes, but his lips twitched. So she slipped the button out of its loop and slid her fingers past his underwear to grip him.

Needless to say, the crowd went wild. Stryker's cock pulsed in her hand, pre-come coating her palm as she stroked him up and down. He raised an eyebrow at her as if in challenge. He wasn't stopping her, so Glitter decided to just go with the flow.

Keeping her hand in his pants, she slowly walked around him, letting her body brush against him and her hips sway so that the crowd got glimpses of the jeweled butt plug. His eyes were on her, a challenge there she couldn't ignore.

Very slowly, she sank to her knees in front of him, spreading her knees wide for balance and to give him a view of her very wet, very swollen pussy. She kept her eyes on him as she slid the zipper down, then pulled his cock free of his underwear. Stryker shifted his stance wider, still looking down at her with a predatory gleam in his eyes. Glitter took his cock by the base and dragged her tongue up the length to collect the drop of pre-come oozing from the head.

Cheers and calls of "Suck it! Suck it!" drove her on. Stryker didn't seem bothered in the least being the center of attention. No doubt, he'd done this same scenario many times at club parties. Which made Glitter all the more determined to make this good for him.

Before she could think better of it, she fastened her lips around the head of his cock and slid down as far as she could go. Her hands slid around his hips to grasp his ass, digging her nails into the fleshy globes. Stryker did throw his head back then, to the utter delight of the women at the stage if the sound of their cheers was any indication. Stryker tunneled his fingers through her hair, pulling it into a ponytail at the back of her head so everyone could see her lips circling him as she sucked.

The party on the second tier of Salvation's Angels went wild. They rarely got a show like this. Glitter had been there two years as a dancer, and she could only remember three such instances. All were with paid performers. All were good, but she wanted her and Stryker to be better.

She continued several minutes, getting into the act, not worrying about being messy. She was enjoying herself, giving her man head in front of a crowd of rowdy -- and likely drunk -- spectators.

"Don't get any ideas, guys," the DJ said with a chuckle. "Everyone's favorite Angel is very taken. Don't believe me? Ask the guy she's currently sucking. He'll tell you. Only, I imagine you won't like the telling." Raucous laughter all around. The "suck it" chant picked up steam then with everyone around the stage chanting and demanding she continue. But Stryker must have had other plans.

He pulled Glitter to her feet by her hair. A collective groan went up as everyone likely thought the show was over.

"Make him come!" someone shouted.

"Make her come!" That from a woman somewhere in the same vicinity, followed by more laughter and cheers.

Stryker took her mouth then, a rough and possessive display of his dominance. "You into this? You trust me?"

She grinned up at him before turning to one of the girls standing next to the stage holding a glass of what Glitter hoped was whisky. She reached for the glass, which the woman happily handed over. Glitter shot it with a gasp, then looked up at Stryker. "With my heart, body, and soul."

"Good. 'Cause I'm not stoppin' till you come right here in front of everyone."

She licked his lip before biting the bottom one and stretching it out. "You gonna fuck me?"

"Damned straight. Every fuckin' hole you got, baby. And I'm fillin' you full of cum when I do."

Glitter's eyes rolled back, she was so turned on. Could she really do this? The whisky helped, but this was a bit over the top. She was on full display, though she was used to the outfit. The erotic jewelry. The full attention on her body. The only difference was Stryker -- her man -- was going to show every man in the place what he'd never have. And he was going to prove how much Glitter loved him fucking her. This was as possessive as it got. A caveman fucking his woman in full view of anyone who thought to take what was his.

He spun her around. Thankfully, Glitter was used to moving in the awkward shoes. The heels put her at the perfect height for him to do as he pleased with her. Which meant he pushed his cock between her legs, sliding it in and out between her thighs so the head poked through her labia jewelry for all to see. His hands rested on her hips, and Glitter gripped his wrists to hold her balance.

"Easy," Stryker murmured at her ear. "I got you baby. You sure you're good with this?"

"Do it," she hissed, widening her stance. "Do it!"

Stryker slid his cock back until it tucked against her entrance. He pushed slightly until the head stretched her pussy just enough to make her suck in a breath. The crowd seemed to do the same. Then Stryker slid home, and everyone around them let up a collective cheer.

Several men and women with phones recorded the event, some yelling, "Oh, my God! He's really fucking her!"

Another yelled, "Dude! Get over here! You gotta see this shit!"

Glitter just closed her eyes with a smile and wound her arms around his neck behind her, hanging on as he thrust in and out of her nearly in time with the music. Her tits shook with his thrusts, as did the gems on the chain between her legs. The butt plug made Stryker seem so much bigger with the space it took inside her. Which made her replay his words to her. Would her really take her ass? Here? Did she want him to? She thought she just might.

One of Stryker's hands found her nipple, and he tugged and twisted the puckered flesh around the clamp she'd applied. Gently, he stretched the nub by pulling on the delicate chain dangling there. More cheers as he continued to fuck her, never missing a beat.

Glitter was so turned on, she knew she could come with the slightest breeze across her clit. But Stryker steadfastly avoided touching it. His clever fingers rubbed over her bare mound, but he spread them to slide down either side of her clit instead of over it. Still, his fingers came away covered in her juices, and he fed them to her. Glitter sucked his fingers eagerly, thrusting back with her hips as much as she could to get him to fuck her faster. Harder. She was rapidly approaching that place only Stryker could take her. The place where she begged and pleaded with him to fuck her. To make her come. To come inside her!

Just as her legs were turning to rubber and she was afraid she might collapse right there, someone slid a barstool with a back on it in front of her on the stage. Glancing around, she saw two of the dancers waving at her over their shoulders as they retreated backstage. Stryker wasted no time, spinning her back around to face him, then lifting her onto the stool. Thank God it was one of the big, sturdy ones with a wide seat, because Stryker lifted her up and spread her legs, kneeling down to suck her cunt and flick her clit briefly before standing before her once again.

Glitter cried out when his tongue brushed her clit, but it wasn't enough to get her off. Something she had no doubt he knew. Spreading her thighs wide, he hooked his arms around them, pulling her to the edge of the seat so he could once again sink his cock into her.

Stryker fucked her. Right there. In front of God and everyone. And Glitter could not have been happier. Her pussy was sopping wet. She could feel her juices dripping down to pool in the leather of the cushion against her cheeks. He was magnificent! The muscles of his chest stood out starkly with his exertion, and his abs rippled with every movement. Long, thick veins crawled up his arms, and the muscles flexed as he gripped her, moved her. All around her Glitter could hear people urging Stryker on. Some were vulgar, others just enjoying the show. To her utter surprise, she was thriving on this. The scent of sweat, alcohol, and sex filled the air. Different fragrances of perfume accented it all. But her eyes were on Stryker. Her magnificent biker. He could be rough and dangerous, cruel when crossed. But he was her protector. Her lover. He must have known she needed this, because he'd thrown all in when she'd shoved her hand down his pants. She loved him all the more.

Finally, with one last thrust, he grunted before pulling her to her feet and turning her around again.

"Taking this fuckin' perfect ass now. You ready, baby?"

"Oh, yeah," she panted. "I'm fuckin' ready!"

Stryker took him time, rubbing and playing with the little plug in her ass while the men and women around them cheered and yelled. Stryker seemed to be encouraging them, involving them in the action about to take place. Slowly, carefully, he pulled the plug until the widest part stretched her. He held it there for a long time. Glitter let out a sharp cry. Not because it hurt, but because it felt so fucking delicious she needed to come. Which reminded her Stryker still hadn't let her come.

"Stryker!" She couldn't contain her scream as sweat broke out over her body. That made their audience even more raucous. They cheered and chanted, "Fuck her ass! Fuck her ass!" over and over. Glitter grinned back at Stryker as he finally pulled out the plug and dropped it on the stage floor.

"You ready?"

"Make me come," she cried.

His low chuckle warmed her insides. "Not until I'm ready to come. The longer I hold you back, the better this will be for you." That was so like Stryker. Looking out for her pleasure and making sure she got as much as he could wring out of her.

Then, slowly, ever so slowly, he pushed the head of his cock inside her ass, letting her adjust to each delicious inch. Glitter pushed back against him as hard as she could. She didn't want slow. She wanted hard and fast.

"Easy!" he snapped. "You'll hurt yourself."

"I'll hurt you if you don't fuckin' get on with it and make me come!" Before she realized what she was doing, she'd bared her teeth and actually hissed at him. The women all seemed to love that.

Stryker just gripped her hips and started giving her what she wanted. With each second, his pace quickened and his grip tightened. Her ass stretched and burned with each stroke, but it was a good feeling. She leaned on the stool as he pounded into her. She gripped the back of it so the thing didn't scoot along the stage, because Stryker wasn't moving. He gripped her tightly and had planted his feet, fucking her with his considerable strength.

It wasn't long before she felt his cock swelling inside her. Glitter whipped her head around, reaching behind her to grip one thick wrist. Stryker batted her away, swatting her ass several times as he continued to fuck her without missing a stroke. Then he gripped both her upper arms and pulled her off the stool. Using her arms as leverage, he fucked her ass mercilessly for several moments. Then he let go of her arms, sliding one of his around her waist, the other down to her clit. He pinched lightly, rubbing it between his fingers as he commanded loudly, "Come for me, Glitter. Come for your Master!"

She did. With a scream that was long and loud, Glitter came. Her ass squeezed Stryker's cock with each spasm until he too yelled a great bellow to the ceiling and emptied himself inside her. Glitter could feel his cum bathing her insides, then dripping down her inner thigh. Stryker squeezed her so tightly, she couldn't breathe for several seconds. Then, gradually, he loosened his hold. His heart beat as wildly as hers did. The audience around them erupted into more cheers and applause. Glitter giggled as Stryker held her against his chest. The hand at her waist slipped up her body to circle her vulnerable throat.

"You're mine, Glitter. I'll never let another man have you. And don't think I'm not fully aware of the spectacle I've just made of you. But don't worry. My brothers will help protect you, though I doubt you'll be able to walk in here without people wanting a repeat performance."

She just sighed. "I loved every second," she whispered, pulling him down to kiss her once. The girls backstage brought her a robe to put on while Stryker pulled up his pants and fastened them.

Glitter turned to wave at the crowd…

And froze.

There. At the very end of the runway. A big, beefy man stood.

"Butcher," she whispered. Then she watched in horror as he pulled out a gun and aimed it at her.

Chapter Ten

Stryker heard her horrified whisper and followed her gaze to the big man taking aim at Glitter with that Smith and Wesson. There was no way he could get to the son of a bitch before Butcher shot Glitter. The only thing he could do was yell, "Gun!" before tackling Glitter to the floor and shielding her with his body.

The gun went off and Stryker jerked, tensing as he waited for the inevitable pain. But nothing came. Horrified screams and shrieks sounded all around him, but there wasn't a second shot. Or even sounds of a struggle. Had the bastard scurried out of the club with the flow of the crowd? Because, yeah. Everyone was leaving en masse. Club shootings were something people never quite recovered from.

What he saw both surprised and angered him. Stryker turned to one of the club girls crouching over Glitter. "Stay with her. Do not leave this stage unless me or another Bane member tells you to." He didn't wait to see if he was obeyed.

Stryker hurried to the end of the runway to find exactly what he suspected he'd find. Butcher lay in a heap on the floor. Blood pooled around him where his head should have been. Over him stood El Segador and Tobias. Both men looked positively void of emotion. Stryker knew Tobias enough to know his brother was debating on whether or not to kill El Segador and dump him on Black Reign's door for the other man bringing a gun into Bane's club.

"I apologize, Stryker. I know you wanted him alive, and I'd intended to deliver him to you. Unfortunately, I found him too late. I was across the room when I spotted him. I doubt either of us could have reached him in time to prevent him from shooting your woman. Or you." He didn't acknowledge Tobias in any way.

Stryker nodded. "He had a bead on her. I didn't have my gun." He frowned. "Why didn't the brothers see him?"

"I'm looking into that," Tobias muttered. Beside him, Lock was texting like mad. "We can't even find where he entered the fuckin' building! He wasn't at the back or side entrance. No one saw him at the front either."

"He'd disguised himself," El Segador offered, pointing to the black trench coat lying several feet away. "Look for that stupid leather trench. Fucking cliché."

It took Lock a few minutes of working on his tablet with the security cameras before he found it. "There," he said sharply, tapping the screen. He shoved it at Stryker, who took it. Sure enough, just like El Segador said, Butcher slipped into the club. How a man that big had managed to make himself that short was beyond Stryker. He'd worn a wig of long grey hair. Instead of drawing the eye, the image repelled it. Kind of like a homeless person you don't want to notice might. No one wanted to see him, so they didn't. At least, no one who was supposed to be looking noticed him.

"If you knew who he was, why'd you let him get that close to Glitter?"

El Segador raised his hands in a defensive gesture. "I didn't notice him at first either. I followed him here, but lost him briefly in the crowd. It must have been when he changed. I probably wouldn't have found him at all if you hadn't yelled about the gun. That's when I found him again."

"Stryker?" Glitter was walking slowly down the runway.

"Don't come any closer, baby. Go backstage. I'll be right there."

She nodded and did as he instructed without question. Stryker couldn't help but smile. She'd done exactly what he told her to do without question or hesitation. Just like he'd hoped. She was probably very upset -- who wouldn't be? -- but maybe this would go a long way toward proving he could and would take care of her in every situation.

"Security's clearing out the building," Tobias said. "We need to clean this and play it off like some kind of prank."

"Leave that to me," El Segador said. "By the end of the evening, even those who might have gotten a clear shot on their phone, or got splattered with blood will question if it was real or a stunt."

"You're the one who shot the fucker," Stryker growled, advancing on El Segador. It wasn't anything personal, Stryker just didn't fucking like the man. "Way I see it is you owe us that. Don't think you can use this as leverage."

"You know, not everyone is out to fuck you over, Stryker. I told you. El Diablo wants peace among our clubs. He thinks we can help each other in ways that will benefit all of us. Besides, you don't honestly believe he'd do anything to jeopardize his relationship with his daughter, do you?"

"That's the only reason Thorn's willing to tolerate Black Reign so close to Salvation's Bane territory. But know, that can change."

El Segador just shrugged. "We have no intention of getting in your way. We have formed a relationship with the Shadow Demons, and they have a good relationship with Bane and Bones. El Diablo has every intention of proving he can be an asset to everyone." He holstered his weapon before continuing. "Talk to Azriel Ivanovich. He knows El Diablo. He can tell you the long and short of it. El Diablo isn't a saint. But he's a man of his word with his own moral code he follows to the letter."

"We'll see," Stryker said. But he didn't question the Reaper any more. Instead, he went to find his woman.

* * *

Waiting sucked. Especially when she'd nearly lost Stryker. When she'd seen Butcher standing there, she knew he was going to kill her. She also knew that Stryker would never let that happen, so Butcher would kill Stryker instead. She had no idea who'd shot Butcher and didn't much give a damn. All that mattered was that Stryker was safe.

The second he entered the dressing room, Glitter jumped up and threw herself into his arms. "I was so scared!"

"I know, honey. I'm sorry. I should have been paying more attention to our surroundings, or, at the very least, made sure the brothers had our backs."

"But they were all there! When everyone was leaving after Butcher was shot, I saw the boys in the crowd. They were all around us."

"Yeah, but they weren't looking for Butcher specifically, and he slipped in with a gun. Which should never have happened. El Segador either, but I can't bitch about him when he saved our lives."

She clung to him for long moments. Stryker took her to a nearby couch and sat. Most of the girls had cleared out, knowing the night was over. They also knew to deny knowing anything if asked. They'd all worked for Angels long enough to know that Bane sometimes operated on the shady side. The less seen, the better.

"What happens now?" Glitter asked.

"We go home. Back to the clubhouse, at least. Tomorrow, assuming El Segador does his part and cleans up this mess, we can head back to my place. For now, though, it's the best place to protect you."

Once back at the clubhouse, Stryker showered with her. Stryker seemed to need to inspect every single inch of her body. It wasn't sexual at first, but it ended up that way once he'd satisfied himself she was, indeed, unscathed. They made love and talked about what happened on stage.

"I've never even contemplated anything like that before."

Stryker chuckled. "Well, I can't promise I'll ever do it again, but it was fun."

"Yeah. Pretty wild. I doubt people will stop talking about it for a good long while. I've already gotten calls and texts from the Angels telling me I've set the bar too high. Much as they could tell I enjoyed myself, they weren't even trying to compete with me."

"Doubt anyone could compete with you when you're that far gone." He carefully rinsed her skin, running his rough palms over her in a lazy caress. "You're fucking amazing when you come."

"You're fucking amazing when you make me come. But, I swear, one of these days you're gonna keep me on the edge just a little too long and I'm gonna shank you."

Stryker's warm chuckle filled her with happiness. His hug was so comforting and reassuring.

Loving. Glitter loved those feelings, and knew she'd always get them from Stryker.

Cleaned and in bed, Glitter laid her head on Stryker's chest. "I never thought I'd end up with you," she whispered. "But I'm so glad I did."

"Me too, baby. You're perfect for me."

"You're perfect for me, too."

"Will Butcher's club try to get revenge? Kiss of Death?"

"Don't know. I guess it depends on how much they know and how much El Segador puts the fear of El Diablo into them. Still don't know what he did with that fucker Rat Man."

"Do you trust El Segador?"

"Not as far as I can throw him. But, so far, he's been straight with us. I get the feeling he's a lot like he said El Diablo is. Got his own moral code. May not be lily white, but he believes it and follows it to the letter."

"Hmm. I know someone else like that."

Stryker gave an exasperated sigh. "What you tryin' to say?"

She giggled. "I'm saying you don't like him because he's like you. Probably the same reason Thorn and all the others don't like him or El Diablo."

"Ain't sayin' you're wrong." There was a beat of silence before he added, "Ain't saying you're right, either."

Glitter snuggled closer to him, kissing his chest before settling again. "You guys'll figure it out. I have faith."

"We will."

"Stryker?"

"Yeah, baby?"

"You know I love you. Right?"

He squeezed her tightly, kissing the top of her head. "Yeah, baby. I love you, too. I love you, too."

Marteeka Karland

Erotic romance author by night, emergency room tech/clerk by day, Marteeka Karland works really hard to drive everyone in her life completely and totally nuts. She has been creating stories from her warped imagination since she was in the third grade. Her love of writing blossomed throughout her teenage years until it developed into the totally unorthodox and irreverent style her English teachers tried so hard to rid her of.

Marteeka at Changeling: changelingpress.com/marteeka-karland-a-39

Changeling Press E-Books

More Sci-Fi, Fantasy, Paranormal, and BDSM adventures available in e-book format for immediate download at ChangelingPress.com -- Werewolves, Vampires, Dragons, Shapeshifters and more -- Erotic Tales from the edge of your imagination.

What are E-Books?

E-books, or electronic books, are books designed to be read in digital format -- on your desktop or laptop computer, notebook, tablet, Smart Phone, or any electronic e-book reader.

Where can I get Changeling Press E-Books?

Changeling Press e-books are available at ChangelingPress.com, Amazon, Apple Books, Barnes & Noble, and Kobo/Walmart.

ChangelingPress.com

Printed in Great Britain
by Amazon

36016565R00129